Hawley Smart

Long Odds

A Novel. Vol. I

Hawley Smart

Long Odds
A Novel. Vol. I

ISBN/EAN: 9783337045494

Printed in Europe, USA, Canada, Australia, Japan

Cover: Foto ©Andreas Hilbeck / pixelio.de

More available books at **www.hansebooks.com**

LONG ODDS.

VOL. I.

a

EDINBURGH:

COLSTON AND COMPANY

PRINTERS.

BY

HAWLEY SMART,

AUTHOR OF

'BREEZIE LANGTON,' 'A FALSE START,' 'CLEVERLY WON,'
'THE OUTSIDER,' 'THE MASTER OF RATHKELLY,'
ETC., ETC.

IN THREE VOLUMES.

VOL. I.

LONDON:

F. V. WHITE & CO.,

31 SOUTHAMPTON STREET, STRAND, W.C.

———

1889.

CONTENTS.

——o——

ERRATA.

VOL. I.

age 2, line 4, for 'have to save,' read '*came* to save.'
  „ 10, „ 13, for 'lnck's view,' read 'luck's *vein*.'
  „ 12, „   9, for 'salon de jue,' read 'salon de jêu.'
  „ 16, „ 16, for 'couldn't say,' read 'could *not* say.'
  „ 21, „   9, for 'to Cuxwolds,' read '*in* Cuxwolds.'   ⌐S⸢
  „ 76, „   7, for 'Staples,' read 'Stubber.'
  „ 121, „   3, for 'Xaxartes,' read '*the Jaxartes*.'
  „ 124, „ 20, for 'of the tribes,' read '*with* the tribes.'
  „ 212, „   8, for 'a good year,' read '*near a* year.'
  „ 215, „   4, for 'knew you had,' read '*know* you *have*.'
  „ 243, „ 14, for 'they,' read '*our people*.'

LONG ODDS.

LONG ODDS.

—o—

CHAPTER I.

TAKE CARE OF DAMOCLES.

A GLORIOUS night. The moon, pale re-
gent of the sky, with all her glittering court,
is marching like an army through the
heavens. The numberless lights of Cairo
twinkle brightly, and the cigars glow like
fire-flies under the verandah of Shepheard's
Hotel. Just visible from the lounging-
chairs there, an unusually brilliant gleam
of light catches the eye, evidently pro-
ceeding from some large building which is
garishly illuminated. From that spot, at

VOL. I.   A

that time of night, the most striking object perhaps in the city of the Khedive.

'So you're getting pretty tired of the place you have to save, Jack, eh?'

'Yes,' replied the Honourable Jack Cuxwold of her Majesty's —th Lancers. 'Before Tel-el-Kebir the certainty that we had work before us kept us going. Then the ride down here was glorious, a match against time, whether we reached Cairo in time to save the city.'

'Yes,' said Flood, 'from all accounts you weren't an hour too soon. Arabi's defeated troops would have fired and sacked it in another four-and-twenty-hours.'

'Just so,' replied Jack Cuxwold. 'I fancy that's what would have taken place. Defeated soldiery "out of hand" would probably treat a wealthy city in that way.'

'Well, it's all over now; and I suppose you'll be soon coming home again?'

'Not a chance of our coming home for ever so long,' retorted Cuxwold; 'and as or its being all over, I very much doubt that. We've pooh-poohed the Madhi, and there being no European troops engaged in it, haven't paid much attention to the annihilation of Hicks' column; but these Arabs are on the boil, and when a fellow calls himself a prophet, if they only take him up, there's no saying where their fanaticism may not carry them.'

'Exactly!' said Flood. 'And I can fancy these fellows thinking a raid from their own sandy deserts into Lower Egypt, in the name of religion, a very profitable speculation. By the way, you were in luck at dinner. That was a deuced pretty girl you contrived to sit next.'

'She was, Master Alec, and very pleasant to talk to besides.'

'Did you make out her name and belongings?'

'She is a Miss Bramton,' replied Cuxwold; 'and that little dark man who sat next her was her uncle. They rather puzzled me. She was as ladylike a girl as you would meet anywhere; but, hang it, I can't make him out.'

'Hardly looked a gentleman,' rejoined Flood.

'No,' said the other, 'whatever he is, he's not that. From what Miss Bramton told me, I gathered that they had come abroad for the benefit of her uncle's health. He is delicate in the chest, and has fled from the rigour of an English winter.'

'Then they're settled here for some time?'

'I suppose so. Miss Bramton told me that they had no intention of leaving till the winter was well over.'

As has been gathered from the previous conversation, the Honourable Jack Cuxwold, second son of the Earl of Ranksborow, was a dragoon, whose regiment had formed part of the original expedition to Egypt. He had been present at the battle of Tel-el-Kebir, and then joined in Stewart's dashing ride to Cairo. Since then he had been kicking his heels about that city, and was now fain to confess that he was most heartily sick of it. He had been up the Great Pyramid, done the Mosques, seen the Sphinx, ransacked the Bazaars, assisted in getting up divisional races, and, in short, to use his own words, had thoroughly exhausted the Khedive's capital. But he knew there was no prospect of getting away, for with Gordon shut up in Khartoum, and the storm clouds of battle gathering in the desert, no man in health could think of applying for leave. Alec Flood was an old friend of his whom he had come across two or three days before, and with whom this evening he had been dining at Shepheard's Hotel. Flood was one of those men, whom you always do come across, blessed with a comfortable income and a restless disposition ; he literally 'wandered up and down upon the earth.' As for his friends, it did not signify what part of the world they had betaken themselves to, they were always prepared to see Alec Flood turn up in his usual listless fashion. He never seemed to know where he was going, and, what was very exasperating to people of ordinarily well-regulated minds, he never seemed to care.

If he was late for train or steamer, going
to such and such a place, he would get
into the next, perfectly regardless of what
its destination might be. 'What does it
matter?' he said upon one of these occasions; 'I haven't made up my mind, you
see, where to go, but I'm quite determined
to go for the present.'   Cairo amused him,
it was not that he hadn't done it all before, but he had met Cuxwold and two or
three other old friends, and so had resolved
to pull up there for a little.   Unmarried,
and with no profession, he was free to roam
wheresoever he would.   Like Ulysses,
he had seen men and cities, and could dis-
course pleasantly of both, and was cordially welcomed in all such society as he
affected; but on this point he was somewhat fastidious, and by no means to be
beguiled by all cards of invitation.

   'I say,' exclaimed Cuxwold at length,
'we can't spend the whole evening in this
drowsy old verandah; what do you say
to coming over there?' and he jerked his
head in the direction of the building that

shone out so brilliantly against the lights of Cairo.

'Anything to see much?' rejoined the other sententiously.

'Well, a music hall is a music hall,' rejoined Jack Cuxwold. 'It's not so entertaining as the Oxford, still one hears a good song sometimes; and they've a girl there who warbles French *chansons* of the Therése type rather archly. At all events, it is better fun than sitting here.'

Alec Flood said nothing, but rose and prepared to accompany his mercurial guest. Left to himself, he would have smoked passively as an Oriental for the next hour or two, and then retired to bed; but the restless Anglo-Saxon blood of Jack Cuxwold rebelled against such passive enjoyment.

'Come on,' he exclaimed, 'it's no distance; and though the streets of Cairo are not policed like those of London, yet nobody ever presumes to interfere with our insular race in any way.'

'No,' rejoined Flood, laughing; 'the conquerors stalk abroad with much majesty at present. It isn't till later on that the conquered avenge their wrongs by midnight assassination.'

Thus jesting, the two young men left their hotel, and made their way to this last exotic of Western civilisation newly grafted on the East. The music hall was, as Cuxwold had explained, of very ordinary type, differing but little from the conventional London entertainment. Only in this wise, that there was a considerable amount of French singing introduced into it. Flood and Cuxwold were perhaps more amused by the queer *mélange* of the audience than in anything they saw upon the stage. The seemingly congregation of all nationalities present, from the Frank in light tweeds to his brother in evening costume; from the Greek of the Levant to the Armenians; from the scarlet fezzed officer of the Egyptian army to the undress of his British compeer. Eastern dresses of all kinds were scattered amongst the audience.

The hall was crowded, and, needless to say, hot.

They had been there for about an hour, and the mercurial Cuxwold was already beginning to doubt whether the game was worth the candle, when they were accosted by a slim dark man of unmistakable Jewish physiognomy, who, in somewhat indifferent English, said,—

'Ah, pouf! Gentlemen, this place is something too hot. What would you think of adjourning to a little establishment that I know of? Ha! we get there something cool to drink, and a leetle amusement. Ha! we see the leetle ball go round and round, we back the colour, we fill our pockets, we rinse our throats; ah, peste! it is more amusing than this place. What say you, gentlemen? Will you stroll across to the establishment of my friend? It is close by. All the best gentlemen of Cairo look in there.'

'Gambling-house tout,' said Flood, in an undertone.

'No doubt,' rejoined Cuxwold; 'still

this is deuced dull.   Suppose we go, Alec,
and look in for half an hour, just to see
how they manage these things in the
East.'

'All right, old man,' rejoined Flood ;
'but a gambling-house is a gambling-
house, whether you see it in the East or
in the West.   However, I don't suppose
that you or I will hurt ourselves much at
it.   I am good to go if you like.   Show
us the way in,' he said, turning to their
new acquaintance, 'and we will see if we
are in luck's view to-night.'

They emerged from the music hall
under the guidance of their new friend,
and, crossing the road, plunged at once
into the labyrinth of small streets that run
at the back of the Great Square, till their
guide stopped at a low doorway, over
which, as has been the fashion of such
dens from time immemorial, their blazed
a brilliant fanlight.   A tap at the door,
and the portal was at once opened, and
their mentor led the way into a narrow
passage which opened into a brilliantly

lighted room, wherein a roulette table, surrounded by a throng of eager speculators, was in full swing.

'A queer crowd, by Jove! Jack; some villainous faces as ever I saw,' whispered Flood.

'Yes,' replied the other; 'and look, Alec, I'm blessed if there isn't our invalid. There's Bramton punting, if I know anything about it, like a man who means business.'

'Ah, gentlemen,' exclaimed their conductor, 'never mind that just now; you will allow me to be your guide. I am well known here. I think just a quail *en aspic* and a glass of champagne before we battle the enemy.'

'Right you are,' rejoined Cuxwold; 'I've a prodigious thirst on me.'

'It strikes me we have met before, my friend,' said Alec Flood, as they followed the stranger into an inner room, where a liberally-furnished supper-table was laid out. 'I can't quite recollect where.'

'Impossible, monsieur,' interposed the

stranger. 'I have an excellent memory for faces, and, monsieur will pardon me,' he continued, with a low bow, 'his is not one that we—ah, what you call it?—forget.'

He called to the attendants, and Cuxwold and Flood were speedily supplied with an excellent supper, washed down with equally good wine. That finished, they at once adjourned to the *salon de jue.*

'Now, messieurs,' said their guide, laughing, 'give me a lead. I never do right myself. I will follow your game, gentlemen.'

It was the ordinary roulette as played at Monte Carlo or any other similar establishment; but the eager faces and glittering eyes of the gamblers showed that the play was deep. There was all the silence that would characterise a London card-room, when the battle waged fierce, and if luck went against them, ruin ere daybreak stared some of the combatants in the face. But these Easterns cannot control their physiognomies like the children of the West,

and, though nothing but a smothered ex-
clamation or low ejaculation of triumph
escaped their lips, the flashing eyes and
flushed faces showed that the intoxication
of gambling was boiling in their veins.

'A run on the red,' whispered Flood ;
' best follow that as far as the colour goes.
Back the numbers to suit your own
fancy.'

Once more did the ball go circling
round, and again did the croupier assever-
ate that red was the successful colour. It
speedily became evident to Flood that
what he had first deemed deep play all
round was pretty nearly confined in this
instance to Bramton, who had been evidently losing heavily, was backing black
with dogged persistency, and was evidently
equally unfortunate in his selection of the
numbers. His face was cool and impas-
sive, but there was an angry light in his
eyes. As Flood and Cuxwold could see,
he kept on increasing his stake after every
rebuff. Once more did the ball spin round,
and as it slowly hesitated which parti-

tion to dribble into, the croupier, either accidentally or by design, touched the board with his hand.

'Foul play, by G—d!' shouted Bramton, springing to his feet. 'No such run as this was ever brought about by fair means; that thief can pull the strings as he likes. I'll have back every shilling he has won of me.'

In an instant all was confusion. The men of that motley crew not only snatched up their own stakes, but in some instances perhaps as much of their neighbour's as they could lay hands on. The quiet of the chamber was broken, and the room rang with a perfect polyglot of blasphemy. The myrmidons of the establishment, of course, gathered round the bank, and well they might, for there were those in that precious crew who reckoned little of how money was come by.

'Disgorge, you scoundrel!' screamed Bramton. 'If you don't return me the money you've robbed me of, I bring the whole place about your ears. I pay up when I lose; but I'll be hung if I'll submit to being robbed,' and, in the excitement of the moment, he sprang at the croupier

For a minute or two the *mêlée* seemed about to be general, and at all events a sharp struggle took place around the bank. Cuxwold and Flood half fought half pushed their way to the scene of action. Suddenly a shriek rang through the room, followed by a cry of 'I am stabbed!' The crowd fell back, and Bramton reeled out of the *mêlée*, bathed in blood, and fell fainting on the floor. In an instant the two Englishmen were at his side. Cuxwold raised his head, and Flood, who in his wanderings had acquired some slight knowledge of surgery, tore open the wounded man's waistcoat only to discover two deep gashes in his chest from which the blood was welling. The tragic ending of the affair seemed to have sobered all those present. They had meddled with an Englishman—meddled with him even to

his death—and there was an obvious
desire on the part of the company to
depart as quickly and privily as might
be. A few minutes and the house was
cleared of all save the wounded man,
Cuxwold, Flood, and its proprietors; and
these latter seemed in much perturbation
at the untoward occurrence. Cuxwold
noticed that the gentleman who had introduced them was amongst those who
had disappeared. He had seen him just
before the commencement of the fray,
apparently staking his money on the
game; but whether he had taken any
part in the scrimmage, or when he disappeared, Jack couldn't say.

'It's no use,' gasped the wounded
man; 'there's nothing much to be done
for me. I've got my gruel, and I know
it. Give me a glass of something, just
to keep me going for a few minutes
while I say what I've got to say. You're
Englishmen, both of you, aren't you?'

Flood nodded assent as he rose to his
feet.

'No,' cried the dying man, as Flood turned towards the door; 'doctors are of no use. I shall be gone before they can get here.'

'I regret to say that, Mr Bramton, I agree with you,' replied Flood gravely. 'I am only going to get you some stimulant. We will do what we can do to forward your wishes, but I know enough of surgery to warn you that you have no time to lose in telling us what you want.'

'Good chap your pal; but he comes pretty straight to the point, don't he? Well it's best, in cases like mine. Let's see, I've seen your face before. Ah! you're the young chap who was at the hotel, and was so civil to Lucy. She is a good girl that. She and Damocles are the only creatures I care about on earth. What I want you to do is this—is your friend never coming with that brandy, or whatever it is?—I feel so faint.'

'Here he is, here he is,' said Cuxwold softly, as he took the tumbler from

Flood's hand, and held it to Bramton's lips.

The man swallowed it eagerly, and then continued,—

'That's what I want you to see about. Just break it to her. Let her down easy. Poor girl, she does care a bit about her old uncle; and then, you see, gentlemen, she's all alone here in a foreign land, and don't know the hang of things. If you'll just put matters straight for her. Manage all about this row; take her passage for England, and all that. There's plenty of money; Dick Bramton ain't dying a pauper by any means. Give me some more brandy. Thanks; that'll do. Will you promise to do what I ask, gentlemen? Don't say more about this than you can help. Say I'm dead, stabbed in the streets, anything. Give her my love. Where am I?—it's getting dark. Tell her to take care of Damocles. I wonder what time it is? I feel awfully sleepy. It's hard, too, with the winner of the Derby in your stable;' and with those words

Dick Bramton fell back upon the cushions
they had laid on him, and seemed to
sleep.

Slowly the blood flowed from the wound,
and trickled over the carpet, in spite of all
Flood's efforts to stanch it. A quarter of
an hour, a slight twitching of the mouth,
a faint fluttering of the eyelids, and Dick
Bramton's spirit had sped.

CHAPTER II.

GOOD-BYE IN REAL EARNEST.

By this time the gendarmes had made their appearance upon the scene, and at once proceeded to take possession of the house and its occupants. Only for Cuxwold's uniform, there was no doubt but both he and Flood would have found themselves in custody; but the guardians of the law were shy of meddling with any one wearing the Queen of England's uniform. The preliminary investigation told nothing. The three men, who avowedly were the proprietors of the house, protested their innocence, and neither Flood nor Cuxwold, although they were fighting their way to Bramton's assistance at the time, had seen who it was that had dealt those fatal blows.

They certainly could formulate no accusation against the three men in question. Cuxwold took a high tone with the officer of gendarmes, and that functionary at once proved subservient and willing to do anything the English captain deemed advisable. He acquiesced at once to Cuxwold's proposal that the body of the dead man should be removed to the hotel at daybreak. He would make every effort to discover the murderer, and exert himself to the utmost of his ability in order that justice should be done ; but it was difficult. They had many of such cases ; so many of these Greeks, Arab dealers, traders, etc., from the Upper Province, carried knives, and were wont to use them freely. He would send down some of his men at daybreak with a hand litter to remove the deceased to Shepheard's Hotel. He would not trouble the gentlemen more than he could help, but it would be necessary that Captain Cuxwold should give evidence before the Cadi, and then with 'plenty salaam' to the two Englishmen, and a fierce whisper to the proprietors of the house, that if plenty of backsheesh were not forthcoming, it would be the worse for them, the man in authority took his departure.

'This is a nice business we've let ourselves in for,' said Flood, in a low tone, as they commenced their vigil o'er the dead. 'I wonder what became of that confounded little Semite. I can't help thinking I've seen that fellow's face somewhere before.'

'Well,' said Jack meditatively, 'I suppose all this would have happened whether we had been here or not. The whole thing passed too quick for us to save this poor fellow; but, for all that, it's as well we were here.'

'As you say so, my dear boy, I suppose it is; but upon my life I can't see it.'

'We can do the poor fellow's last bidding,' said Jack. 'It's better that pretty girl at the hotel should have the thing broken gently to her, instead of hearing of it abruptly. She will want some one, too, to help her about all her arrangements to return home, etc.'

Flood eyed his companion curiously for a moment, and then remarked,—

'True; you are a good fellow, Jack, and always had a touch of chivalry in your nature. Consider me as under your orders in every respect about this affair. I wonder who or what is Damocles—a dog, I suppose?'

'I can tell you all about that,' replied Cuxwold. 'That name reveals a good deal to me about the poor fellow who's gone. I don't do very much in the racing way myself—younger sons can't afford it— but I come, remember, of a regular racing stock. My noble father and Dartree, my eldest brother, are up to their eyes in it. Well, if it's only to see what their horses are doing, I always skim the racing intelligence. Damocles is a two-year-old of whom great things are expected. He was bought for a lot of money last year by Richard Bramton, who is a well-known

racing man—began life, I believe, as a
stable-boy—and who was yesterday one
of the luckiest owners on the turf.'

'Ah! a self-made man?' remarked
Flood.

'Quite so; I never saw him before last
night at dinner, and never dreamt of his
being the man who on the turf they call
" Lucky Dick Bramton." How the deuce
a niece of his is what Miss Bramton is
is somewhat difficult to explain.'

'It is odd,' said Flood. 'She was as
refined, ladylike a looking girl as one
ever came across, and her poor uncle, even
in his last moments, quite justified your
opinion of him as to his not being a
gentleman; he was very rough of speech.'

'Yes,' replied Cuxwold; 'but here are
the first streaks of dawn. Ah! and here
come the gendarmes with their stretchers.'

The gendarmes at once entered the
house, and the remains of poor Dick
Bramton were at once placed reverently
on the stretcher by Cuxwold and Flood.
Under their auspices, the body was borne

back to Shepheard's Hotel, and safely deposited in the dead man's chamber, there to await burial. The proprietor of the hotel was much concerned. Such a thing as the assassination of a guest of his within a mile of his house had never happened before. He could not understand it. When did it take place? But upon this point Cuxwold and his friend were somewhat reticent, preferring at present that the hotel-keeper should believe it to be the result of a street brawl rather than of a *fracas* in a gaming-house.

'Now,' said Jack, 'let's go up to your room. By the time I've made myself a little decent, Miss Bramton, no doubt, will be up, and I've got to tell her then what has happened.'

People rise early in the East. There is not much to induce one generally to sit up in such cities as Cairo. Men will sit up to play under all climes, and under all circumstances. Nothing but the most arbitrary law stops the gambler in his favourite pursuit.

Miss Bramton was up betimes, and flitting about her sitting-room, waiting for her uncle to come to breakfast. They usually took that meal more or less together in their own apartment; but her uncle was habitually unpunctual, and Lucy as often as not had finished breakfast before Dick Bramton put in his appearance. She was just debating in her own mind whether she should ring for that repast, when a servant entered and said that a gentleman wished to see her. To the very natural request of 'What is the gentleman's name?' the waiter produced an envelope, on the back of which was written, 'Captain Cuxwold requests to see Miss Bramton on business of urgent importance.' That Captain Cuxwold was the name of her neighbour at the *table d'hôte* on the previous night Lucy was aware, and though the request was not a little extraordinary, still, from what she had seen of him, she could not but believe that he must have reasonable grounds for making it.

'Tell the gentleman I shall be very glad to see him.'

Another moment and Jack Cuxwold entered the room, feeling, sooth to say, considerably more nervous than was his wont at being shown into a lady's boudoir.

'Good-morning, Captain Cuxwold,' said Miss Bramton. 'The waiter tells me that you wish to see me; but we know how stupid these people at the hotel are. It is far more probable that your business is with my uncle, whose acquaintance seems to me to comprise men of all kinds and conditions.'

'No, Miss Bramton,' returned Jack gravely, 'I regret to say my business is with you. I grieve to say that your uncle was seriously injured in a street fray last night. I was present, and, though I did my best, was unluckily too late to come to his assistance.'

'Uncle Dick hurt!' exclaimed the girl. 'Where is he? I must go to him at once; tell me Captain Cuxwold,' and the dark grey eyes looked keenly into his.

'It's what I've come to do, Miss Bramton. Please be quiet, and sit down, and don't make my task more difficult than it is already. Everything has been done for your Uncle Dick that is possible, and it would be useless your going to him now.'

'Why not?' she exclaimed. 'He may be rough, he may be uncouth, but he has been the best and dearest uncle to me always. He has never grudged any expense if he thought a thing would give me pleasure. If he is seriously hurt, my place is at his bedside; it is trifling with me, Captain Cuxwold, not to tell me where he is. No one can nurse him as well as me.'

'You have misunderstood me, Miss Bramton. I fear I am doing my errand badly. Cannot you understand, there are cases past all nursing?'

'Past all nursing,' repeated Lucy. 'Do you mean to tell me,' she continued slowly, while her eyes dilated and her voice dropped almost to a whisper, 'that my uncle is *dead?*'

'Even so,' rejoined Jack. 'I saw him struck down with my own eyes—was with him to the last—and have brought his dying message to you.'

'Saw him struck down, sir!' exclaimed the girl indignantly; 'and is the man alive who dealt that felon blow, or is he in the hands of the police?'

'He has escaped justice so far, Miss Bramton,' rejoined Cuxwold, in low tones.

'And what were you doing, sir? Did you stand aside and see death dealt out to one of your countrymen without raising your hand? You are a soldier, and a powerful man besides. It surely couldn't be that you were afraid to interfere?'

Cuxwold's face flushed under the undeserved taunt.

'No,' he said quietly, after a moment's hesitation, 'I don't think it was that. It was chance brought me and my friend upon the scene. Your uncle was struck down before we could reach him.'

'Forgive me, I feel that I have done you injustice. I hardly knew what I was saying. You see the shock has come suddenly upon me, and I loved him very dearly; but I must see him. Where is he?'

'There is no difficulty about your see-ing him, Miss Bramton. We watched by him through the night, and brought him here at daybreak. We have laid him in his own room.'

'Take me to him, please,' said Lucy, still struggling with her tears.

Jack Cuxwold silently conducted her to the dead man's chamber, and left her on the threshold. Lucy Bramton walked swiftly to the bed, and gently drew back the sheet. One glance was sufficient. There could be no doubt that the de-stroyer had claimed her uncle. She pressed her lips to the dead man's fore-head, replaced the sheet, and then, fall-ing upon her knees by the bedside, burst into a paroxysm of weeping. The tear-storm did her good, and when some quarter of an hour later she emerged from the silent chamber, her face, though very pale, was calm. Somewhat to her surprise, when she entered the sitting-room, she found Jack Cuxwold seated there.

'I've no wish to intrude upon your grief, Miss Bramton,' said Jack, rising. 'I have only waited to tell you that I will do everything that is necessary about the investigation of this unfortunate occurrence. I will also make every arrangement for the funeral, which, as perhaps you are aware, out here will have to take place at once. I will say no more now, but leave you to collect your thoughts and think over what you wish done. When you want me, you will have nothing to do but to ring the bell and say so. I shall be somewhere about the hotel,' and without waiting for the thanks which Lucy was about to proffer, Jack left the room.

The investigation of the murder proceeded in the leisurely way characteristic of all business in the East. There was no clue to the assassin, and, as was pointed out to Cuxwold, no probability of his being discovered unless a large reward was offered, and as Flood, who knew the East well, observed cynically, 'It will be doubtful whether you get the right man even then, as some of these fellows to obtain money would just as soon swear their fellows' lives away as not.'

Richard Bramton was quietly laid to rest in the English cemetery; and thus terminated the tragedy which was destined to have a singular effect on the future of two of the people indirectly mixed up in it. Lucy Bramton naturally decided to return to England by the very next steamer. Jack Cuxwold took her passage, and even accompanied her by railway to the point of embarkation. As he wished her farewell on the deck of the steamer, Lucy said,—

'I made a shameful accusation against you in the first moment of my agony, but I know you would make every allowance for a grief-stricken girl, and that you have forgiven me. Is it not so?'

'Pray don't mention it,' replied Jack. 'I have forgotten all about it.'

'You have been very kind to me, and if ever you come into Barkshire, I hope you will let papa thank you for all the care you have taken of his daughter.'

'I had no idea you lived in Barkshire,' said Cuxwold.

'We are newcomers in the county,' replied Lucy, 'and know very few people as yet. Good-bye.'

'I am afraid it is good-bye in real earnest now, they've passed the word, "All for shore." Good-bye; I hope you'll have a good passage, and next time I'm in Barkshire I shall come and see you. However, I'm not likely to leave this country at present. Once more, good-bye,' and Jack pressed the little hand extended to him, raised his cap, and disappeared across the gang-way.

CHAPTER III.

THE TELEGRAM.

A LARGE suburban villa of the very best type, for such really is the only way to describe the house, though it stands many miles away from the metropolis, surrounded by grounds which no doubt in spring and summer were extremely beautiful. One could fancy the horse-chestnuts, copper-coloured beeches, and laburnums in all their glory; the great clumps of rhododendrons and azaleas all ablaze; and those trim beds in the parterre, which at the present moment are what the gardeners call 'banked up,' glowing with brilliant flowers, borders of lobelia, golden chain, and low scarlet geranium.   But this bright March morning the hand of winter still holds nature in its grasp, and though the snowdrops and crocuses are beginning to peep above ground, it is as yet far too early for the unfolding of leaves or the song of the birds, except on behalf of those foolish feathered creatures who, like humanity, are too apt to think that one fine day makes a summer.

Pacing up and down the terrace, outside the drawing-room windows, is a stout, pompous, middle-aged gentleman, who, with his shooting jacket thrown back, and his thumbs stuck into the arms of his waistcoat, is contemplating the grounds with an air of patronising approval.   You can read what he thinks in his face.   He is evidently saying to himself, 'Yes, you are mine, and pretty well up to the mark, I believe.   I don't suppose in all Barkshire there's a prettier place than Temple Rising.'

If Mr John Bramton's feelings could have been more thoroughly analysed, his reflection would have been somewhat in this wise,—'Yes, it's a pretty place; it's a dooced good house; they are monstrous nice grounds, and so they ought to be, considering I keep four gardeners to look after 'em. Yes, no doubt it's a nice thing to retire, and to become a country gentle-man, but I'm not sure whether the old villa at Wimbledon wasn't better fun. I used to see my old friends there. Mrs B. and Matilda said they were vulgar. I don't know about that. Mrs B. tells me I'm vulgar sometimes; perhaps I am. I wasn't brought up among Court circles. If I had been, Mrs B. might have been wearing silk gowns, but she'd have had to do it on credit most likely. Well, she and Matilda have got their way. Here I am, John Bramton of Temple Rising, and enrolled amongst the nobility and gentry of Barkshire,—plenty of money in my pockets, best of wine in my cellar, dry champagne and Madeira that I'd back to knock corners off anything the Right Honourable Earl of Ranksborow

can show. Well, as I said before, here
we are, here we are likely to remain, but
the nobility and gentry of Barkshire don't
seem to trouble their heads about us.
It's aristocratic no doubt. We're classed
in the county blue book amongst the
nobs, but that's where it is; we're not
classed among them anywhere else. It's
aristocratic, as I said before, but it's
devilish dull, and what's worse, Mrs B. is
always reminding me of that fact. She
blows me up about it, as if I could make
people call as when I was in the dry
goods' business. We put our best goods
in the window, and if that didn't fetch
customers we couldn't help it. Now, one
can't do that socially. If I got up a
tableau of Matilda in her best frock, and
a small table at her right hand containing
a vase of hothouse roses, and a bottle of
that extra dry champagne, and put it in
the dining-room window, nobody would
see it; and I don't think I should quite
like to propose it to Matilda. She has
a soul above trade, and could never be

brought to see the beauty of a good advertisement.'

John Bramton had made a very considerable fortune in a wholesale dry goods' business in the city. A wary man always, when he began to find business irksome to him, he resolved to retire. He had seen too many of his compeers, who, under similar circumstances, had elected to remain in their firms as sleeping partners, abandoning the guidance of the ship to other hands, and the result bring utter shipwreck in the course of a few years. When he left the helm, he resolved to have no further share in the cargo. He retired to his villa at Wimbledon, and enjoyed himself immensely, running into the city constantly to have a crack with his old friends, and frequently bringing home stout, plethoric, middle-aged gentlemen to dinner.

But this by no means suited the ambitious views of Mrs Bramton and her eldest daughter. As for Lucy, the youngest, as her mother and sister continually told her, she was a poor, mean-spirited little wretch, who had no proper pride or self-respect. Mrs Bramton panted to mix in county society, to give garden parties to which the *élite* of the neighbourhood would be only too anxious to attend. We know the old story, 'Water wears away the stone, and a woman's tongue by degrees will vanquish a man's will.' In utter defiance of his own judgment, John Bramton sold the snug villa at Wimbledon in which the late prosperous days of his life had been passed, and invested in the far more pretentious manor of Temple Rising.

'John, John, here's a telegram just come for you,' exclaimed a stout, very dressy lady, appearing at one of the French windows opening on to the terrace; 'and have you taken any steps about what I told you?'

'Perhaps you wouldn't mind being a little more explicit. You see, my dear, you tell me a good many things.'

'Now, don't be aggravating; you know

what I mean. You must get appointed one of the magistrates of the county. I insist on your being on the bench.'

'It's all very well, Margaret,' replied John Bramton; 'but I can't appoint myself, and what's more, it would not be quite the advantage you expect it to be. Where is this telegram?'

'Don't talk nonsense, John. In attending to your magisterial duties,' continued the lady with great pomposity, 'you would make the acquaintance of all the leading people on this side the county. There's the Earl of Ranksborow, why he lives only four miles from us.'

'Just so, Margaret; but these nobs have a way with them,' replied John Bramton, as he stepped through the window and took the telegram from his wife's hand. 'They would know me on the bench, but not off it.'

As he spoke he tore open the orange envelope, and suddenly exclaimed,—

'Good heavens! it's from Lucy. Poor Dick is dead, and she's coming home by the next steamer. Poor fellow! we haven't seen much of each other of late years. Our ways were so very different.'

'Well, I am very sorry for your brother, John, but I must say the peculiar language he was wont to indulge in always did jar upon my nerves.'

'Poor Uncle Dick,' observed a showy, fashionably-dressed young lady, who was seated in a low chair by the fire, as she laid down the book she was reading ; 'he was dreadfully slangy, and it always puzzled me how Lucy could like going abroad with him. However, he was very kind-hearted.'

'Poor Dick, he was as kind a fellow as ever stepped,' said John Bramton. 'As for his talk, well I suppose it was the slang of his business. Never understood anything about racing myself, though, mind you, I have been to the Derby. Now, you needn't look, Mrs B. 'Twas many years ago, long before I was married. The only thing I remember about it is that I came home with a broken hat and a false nose.'

'Uncle Dick's death must have been very sudden,' remarked Miss Bramton. 'In her last letter, Lucy described him as being so much better, and having quite lost his cough. The telegram, I suppose, tells you nothing, papa.'

'It only says this: "Uncle Dick died suddenly; am coming home by next steamer; particulars by mail." The chances are Lucy will be here almost as soon as her letter.'

'There ought to be a bit of money come your way, John. I should say your brother was a well-to-do man; and he has nobody but you to leave it to.'

'Goodness knows, my dear,' replied John Bramton. 'I never understood that trade of his; but it's lightly come lightly go with all those racing fellows; their pockets are full to-day, and empty to-morrow. No need to speculate to what poor Dick has left behind him or where it goes.'

That the dead man's had been as much a business as his own was a thing you

couldn't possibly have got into John
Bramton's head. In his mind there was
no difference between a race-course and
the tables at Monte Carlo. He really
was as ignorant about turf matters as it
was possible for any man in England to
be ; and that visit to Epsom, when he was
quite a young man, was the sole instance
of his ever being present at a race meeting. He had always regarded his brother
as a perfectly unbusinesslike man, upon
no other grounds than that he got his living in a way utterly unintelligible to him,
John Bramton ; and he honestly thought
that the probabilities were the deceased
had made no will, and left next to nothing
behind him.

But the family at Temple Rising were
destined to be still more astonished when
the post brought in the evening paper. It
had never occurred to the Bramtons that
Uncle Richard was a celebrity in his way ;
on the contrary, he was a relative of whom,
if anything, they were a little ashamed ;
and both John Bramton and his wife,

especially the lady, had always treated
Richard in a more or less patronising way.
Their astonishment was boundless when,
upon opening the *Globe*, they read the
following telegram, dated Cairo,—

'We regret to announce the death here,
under most melancholy circumstances, of
Mr Richard Bramton, a gentleman well
known in turf circles, and who, from the
extraordinary good fortune which attended
him on the race-course, had acquired the
sobriquet of " Lucky Dick Bramton."
The deceased gentleman, it seems, had
found his way into one of those low gam-
bling-houses, which, to our everlasting
disgrace, are still permitted to exist in
this city. It seems a *fracas* arose, in the
course of which some of the foreigners
used their knives freely, and the unfortunate gentleman was so fatally stabbed
that he expired of his wounds within the
hour. The event is calculated to create
great excitement in sporting circles. The
deceased was the owner, though fortun-
ately not the nominator, of Damocles for

his numerous engagements, and this dark youngster has the reputation of being a two-year-old very much above the common.'

'Well,' said John Bramton, 'upon my word, it's very handsome of this newspaper fellow to mention poor Dick in that manner, although, perhaps, on the whole, it would have been better if he had not referred to where his death took place! Murdered, poor fellow! God bless me! what else could he expect, going into such a den as that? Poor Dick, he always was venturesome, and never could resist gambling. It's a bad business, a bad business.'

'It must have been a very unpleasant business for Lucy,' chimed in Miss Bramton. 'How dreadful for her, poor girl, to be mixed up in such a horrible story.'

'Now, look here, Matilda,' said her father, 'what do you mean by "mixed up?" You don't suppose Lucy went with her uncle to that den, do you?'

'I am sure I don't know,' replied Miss Bramton, with a toss of her head.

John Bramton was persistently snubbed by his wife and eldest daughter, and as a rule bore it meekly; but there was one thing which they knew by experience invariably provoked retaliation on his part, and that was any abuse of Lucy. John Bramton was very fond of his youngest child, and never failed to take up the cudgels on her behalf, although too easy-going a man to do so on his own. A day or two more, and, not a little to his surprise, Mr Bramton received a letter from Messrs Drysdel and Pecker, solicitors, informing him that they were the legal advisers of Richard Bramton, and requesting to know if he had received any confirmation of the death of their client, adding that they knew no more than what was reported in the papers; but that, upon making inquiry at the office of the journal in which the original paragraph had appeared, they had been informed that the intelligence had been cabled home by an old and trusted correspondent, and that the editor felt no doubt as to its accuracy.

'You may depend upon it, John,' exclaimed Mrs Bramton, when she heard of this letter, 'that he has left property behind him. A man who has solicitors is sure to be a man of substance, and, of course, they communicate with you as the next-of-kin.'

'You are rather hasty in your conclusions, Mrs B.,' replied her husband. 'Bankrupt firms usually have solicitors. I could fancy poor Dick perpetually wanting a lawyer to get him out of some hobble or other.'

Now this, again, was a perfectly unwarrantable assumption on the part of the elder brother. He had never heard of Dick being in a scrape of any kind ; but, in his complete ignorance of the mysteries of a trainer's calling, he looked upon him as one of those who habitually occupied a delicate position with regard to the police. However, of course, he replied to the letter of Messrs Drysdel and Pecker, informing them that he had had a telegram from his daughter which confirmed the news of her uncle's death, that Miss Bramton was on her way home, and was expected at Temple Rising in a few days. His answer produced another letter from Messrs Drysdel and Pecker, in which they briefly requested to be immediately apprised of that young lady's arrival.

'Suspicious chaps these lawyers; must have evidence that poor Dick is dead. I suppose he fancies that Lucy can swear to it.'

CHAPTER IV.

DICK BRAMTON'S WILL.

THERE was a ringing of bells, and a sound
as if a tornado had swept through the
house, when about a week later Lucy
Bramton, in deep mourning, drove up to
the door of Temple Rising. It was not
in the least that this ostentatious style of
arrival accorded with Lucy's ideas, but her
father and mother had no notion of paying
servitors for nothing. If the man at the
lodge didn't make the bell peal again, and
thereby give due notice to the outside
world that there were visitors at Temple
Rising; if the butler did not throw open
the door with a crash, and make the very
walls resound with the name of those

visitors ; if the very footman did not in some way contrive to pervade the very stairs with the intelligence that Mr and Mrs So-and-so had *done themselves* the honour to call at Temple Rising, they were of no account, and useless in the eyes of Mr and Mrs Bramton. No people these to conceal their light under a bushel ; and if perchance a duke or very much minor light of the peerage should deign to call upon them, they were most distinctly of opinion that it would be good for all Barkshire to know it. Poor Lucy, terribly shocked at the tragedy which, so to speak, had taken place almost under her own eyes, would have crept quietly enough into her own home, if she could have done so, but the henchmen of Temple Rising were much too well-trained for anything of this kind, and before she could clasp her mother's neck, the name of Miss Lucy Bramton was sounded through hall and corridor, and neither the Grand Duchess of Russia, nor the heiress of that mythical monarch Prester John, could have been announced with greater *fanfare* of trumpets. 'Miss Lucy Bramton! Miss Lucy Bramton!' resounds through hall and staircase, and then the slight girlish figure in black is sobbing on the breast of a middle-aged, bald-headed, prosaic-looking gentleman.

'Very, very glad to see you back, my dear!' exclaimed John Bramton. 'It has no doubt been a terrible shock to you and poor Dick. Well, of course, we always knew he carried on anyhow, but I never thought he would make an end of it that way.'

'Once for all, father, understand this,' exclaimed the girl, rapidly releasing herself from his embrace, and drawing her slender figure up to its full height, 'I will listen to no reflections against Uncle Dick. He might be rough, but he was ever to me the kindest and most indulgent of relations; not a whim or caprice of mine that he would not indulge. You are a kind and a dear father to me, but even you have never humoured me in the way

poor Uncle Dick used. How he got into
that wretched place, how he met his doom,
I can't think. I, at all events, can bear
to hear no stones thrown at his memory.
I know what mother is, I know what
Matilda is, let them think as they like,
but please, please father, let them say
nothing against Uncle Dick's memory
before me.'

'No, no ; certainly not, my dear. I'll
tell your mother, and I'll speak to Matilda.
They sha'n't trouble you, my pet,' and
then John Bramton inwardly wondered
what deference to his prohibition would
be accorded by that dictatorial wife of
his.

'It was an awful shock for me when
they told me he was dead. He left me
after dinner, as he said, to smoke a cigar,
as he had done scores of times before.
What induced him to go to the villainous
den at which he met his death, I can't
say. I have been abroad with him often,
and feel sure it was contrary to his usual
habits ; but he's gone. I kissed his dear

face, and I can't bear to hear anything said against him. Let it be, father. He has gone; whatever his faults might have been, don't let me hear of them.'

'Quite right, my child, quite right,' said John Bramton, gently patting the head that nestled on his shoulder. 'I'll do my best, but you are aware that your mother, and, I may say, even Matilda, are a little trying under these circumstances. Good woman, your mother, very good woman, but she will speak her mind, you know; and Matilda, well Matilda takes a little bit after her mamma. I will do my best. I will speak to them; but bless you, Lucy, you know when your mamma is "on the rampage" she can't hold her tongue; and I wouldn't say a word against Matilda for the world; but whenever she marries, I think her husband will come pretty much to the same conclusion. Good women both, my dear, but rather free of speech.'

The third morning after Lucy's return was signalised by the arrival at Temple

Rising of Mr Pecker, junior partner of the firm of Drysdel and Pecker. He was cordially welcomed by Mr Bramton in the first instance, and at once proceeded to unfold the object of his errand.

'We have acted for some years as the legal advisers of the late Mr Richard Bramton. We made his will, which is dated some five years back. It is very simple, and to the best of our belief perfectly incontestable in any court of law. The deceased gentleman was an excellent man of business.'

'What!' exclaimed John Bramton; 'Dick a man of business! Nonsense! don't tell me.'

The lawyer shrugged his shoulders.

'Ah,' he said, 'I see; like many other people you're under the delusion that racing men are not men of business. You are wrong; professional racing men are about the most astute men of business I ever come in contact with. I have considerable experience of them, and remember, I draw a great distinction between racing men and men who go racing.'

'Well, to hear that poor Dick was a man of business beats me!' said John Bramton, evidently in utter amazement at the bare idea.

'You must take my word for it,' said Mr Pecker, smiling. 'You will perhaps also be surprised to hear that he was a man of considerable property. As the greater part of his securities are deposited in our hands, and as we possess a list of those which he thought fit to keep at his bankers, we can speak confidently on this point. Mr Richard Bramton has left behind him about five-and-thirty thousand pounds, besides his racing stud. What that may be worth I have no conception. I have no knowledge of such matters.'

'Five-and-thirty thousand pounds!' exclaimed John Bramton. 'Why I should never have given Dick credit for as many hundreds; and who has he left it all to?'

'He has left everything, the horses in-
cluded, to his niece, Miss Lucy Bramton,
and you are appointed sole executor.   I
have brought the will with me for you
to read; it's very brief, and cannot well
be simpler, with the exception of this
codicil; and about this, I must tell you,
I'm not quite sure.   It says, as you will
see,' and Mr Pecker pointed to the place,
'quite clearly that the horses are to be
run through their engagements.   This, as
far as I understand, means that Miss
Lucy cannot dispose of the stud till such
engagements as have been made for the
various horses have been decided.   Whoever has charge of them will, I presume,
advise her how to manage on that point;
but it is open to question whether she
has the power of selling them before their
engagements have expired.'

'You are aware, Mr Pecker, that my
daughter is a minor, that I consequently
am her natural trustee, and that what is
to be done with those horses will therefore
rest in my hands; and I tell you what it

is, sir, I don't want any time to decide. I know nothing about race-horses, and don't want to. I'm not going to take to gambling at my time of life. Those horses go to the hammer before six weeks are over our heads.

'Ah!' said Mr Pecker, putting his head rather on one side, 'this gives rise to the rather curious question of whether you've the power to act in this way. There is no doubt about the body of the will; but our late client, just before starting on his last unfortunate trip to Egypt, had his will, together with some other papers, back for a night, and has added this codicil himself, without consultation with us. It is a delicate and most interesting point to know whether that codicil implies a wish, or imposes a condition.'

'Condition; nonsense!' exclaimed Mr Bramton. 'You can't make it a condition that I'm to keep an expensive lot of animals that I don't want.'

'Oh, yes, my dear sir; excuse me, that's quite possible. Old ladies are very

apt to provide for favouite cats in that
way. As I told you, I'm not quite prepared to say the codicil does that. You
will have to take counsel's opinion on
it if necessary ; but as you are acting
for your daughter, and I can't suppose
that Miss Lucy would have any desire
to keep on her uncle's stud unless she
was obliged, it would be possible perhaps to treat it as merely a wish ; and
then, my dear sir, it becomes a matter
of simply what deference you mean to
pay to the desire of your deceased
brother.'

'Don't put it in that way!' exclaimed
Mr Bramton. 'Of course I am anxious
to do everything that poor Dick wished,
but he never could have intended that
either Lucy or myself were to take to
horse-racing. Now come into the other
room, and have some lunch.'

'In a few minutes, Mr Bramton, with
pleasure ; but I shouldn't be doing my
duty if I didn't personally read and explain this will to Miss Lucy. It won't

take five minutes, if you will only be good enough to fetch her.'

John Bramton rose, and speedily returned, accompanied by his younger daughter. He had briefly explained the fortune she had come in to, and what she was wanted for. Mr Pecker, on being introduced to her, wasted no time, but proceeded at once to business. He read the will through, codicil and all, and briefly explained to her the doubt which existed in his mind as to which way the codicil was to be regarded, whether as a wish or a condition, winding up with the remark, ' But as this is a matter that lies between you and your father, it is hardly likely to be called into question.' He then briefly congratulated her on her inheritance, looked at his watch, and said,—

' And now, Mr Bramton, if you can, give me something to eat. I've just twenty minutes to spare before starting for the railway station.'

Lucy had made no comment upon the

will, except to acknowledge the lawyer's congratulations. She had hardly opened her lips, but for all that, she had listened very attentively to what Mr Pecker had said to her, more especially with regard to that strange codicil. To say that she had come to any resolve concerning it would be absurd. She did not exactly comprehend as yet what it meant. All she knew was this, that the colt called Damocles was one of her uncle's most cherished possessions, and that his dying message had commended Damocles to her care.

About this period it suddenly dawned upon Her Majesty's Government that a person called the Mahdi was about to occasion trouble in Upper Egypt. Her Majesty's Government, with that grand geographical ignorance that usually characterises it, whether Liberal or Conservative, suddenly awoke to the fact that a place called Khartoum was rather an important city in those parts which it behoved them to hold. Her Majesty's

Government, furthermore, became somehow aware that a person of the name of
Gordon had more knowledge of those
parts than any one living. Further, that
the said Gordon was an officer of considerable distinction, and that, if there
was anything to be done in the way of
saving Khartoum, this was the man to
do it. Government, not particularly clear
about what the especial object was in
saving Khartoum ; not in fact very clear
about the Soudan and Upper Egypt
generally, but hazily aware that the Mahdi
promised to be an uncomfortable fact in
the case, and give trouble generally, at
last gave Gordon a roving commission to
do as he thought best for the pacification
of the Soudan, and then, after the usual
manner of British Governments, having
picked out the very best man for the
work, proceeded to tie his hands in all
possible directions. They took no notice
of what he demanded, although he made
his way promptly to Khartoum ; informed
them at once that it was the key of the

Soudan, and that as long as he held that, let what wild work might go on in the desert, he was the virtual ruler of the country. Government read his despatches, said, 'We have bombarded Alexandria, put down Arabi, taken Cairo; good, it will be time enough now to see about Egypt in another year or two.' Letter after letter, despatch after despatch, came from the grand soldier who had taken upon himself this terrible burden. The errand which the Government had sent him on they now sought to repudiate. They tried to make out that his mission had been of his own seeking; but the gathering roar of the British public at last convinced them that they stood bound to fall by the man they had virtually sent to grapple with the insurrection of the Soudan.

By this time all England was aware that Chinese Gordon was shut up in Khartoum, and was defending himself against swarms of fanatical Arabs. Closely beleaguered though he was, he managed to get despatch after despatch through his myriad foes; and those short pithy despatches never varied in their tenor. 'I can hold my own,' he invariably said, 'till the end of December; that passed, we shall be destitute of food, and I can guarantee no more.' Months still intervening between this and December, but the heat of summer having commenced, and the fall of the Nile having begun, it suddenly occurred to the Government that, however late it might be for an expedition of this kind, the irritation of the British public must be appeased. Utterly deaf to the man they had doomed to destruction, the Government yielded to the political outcry of the country, and summoning all the military experts to their councils, debated as to how Khartoum might be most speedily relieved. That they had probably hit upon the best device to achieve that result is possible; we only know two things, they were too late, and they did not take the route which Gordon, who might be supposed to know something about it, advised.

All this discussion and turmoil as to the relief expedition took place just after Lucy Bramton had come into her inheritance.

CHAPTER V.

THE HELIOTROPE.

A VERY lively club was the Heliotrope, much given to baccarat, poker, and divers games at times not recognised at clubs of greater stability,—one of those mushroom night clubs that spring up and are wont to have the mushroom's ephemeral existence. All London—that is, the ten or twelve thousand people who consider themselves all London—would have unanimously admitted that, to put it mildly, the members of the Heliotrope were a 'lively lot.' It was a club with no architectural pretensions whatever; indeed, the three hundred members who constituted it contented themselves with a roomy first floor off the Strand. The club, indeed, practically consisted of three rooms: the supper-room, card-room, and kitchen. There was much discussion, scandal, and tobacco going on in the supper-room one evening, when a studious member, who had pulled himself together and devoted himself to the mastery of the evening papers, suddenly exclaimed,—

'Hallo, Dart, here's something will interest you!'

'Very glad to hear it,' replied a tall, good-looking young fellow about thirty. 'It's such a godsend when anything does, considering the awful way in which those fellows down at St Stephen's bore us. Can't conceive myself what makes the governor so persistent about my going in for representing the county. Suppose he suffered from it himself in his youth, and thinks it a wholesome chastisement for his first-born. What's your news? If you've found anything in that paper, drawl it out.'

'Only this,' replied the speaker; 'Dick

Bramton has got wiped out in a gambling-house row at Cairo; and considering your father snapped all the yearling books about Damocles when the colt was sold, I thought it might interest you.'

'Interest me; by Jove! I should think it did!' said Lord Dartree. 'I took twenty thousand to three hundred about Damocles once, and the governor took it as often as he could get it. In fact, between us we captured every yearling book there was going. Damocles is entered in the name of his breeder, so that's all right; but what becomes of him is quite another matter. Dick Bramton would have run him as straight as a die. He is an old racing pal of the governor's, and knew he could have any fair share of the plunder that he chose to stipulate for.'

'He'll most likely be sold now, I should think,' observed Anson, the gentleman who had read out the news.

'Suppose he will,' rejoined Lord Dartree. 'I must try and persuade the governor to buy him, though how the deuce we are to lay our hands on ten thousand pounds, or whatever it is they want for him, I'm blest if I know. We have got partridges, we have got stabling, we have got gardens, and no end of a library at Knightshayes, but, my dear Anson, we haven't got any money. Everybody knows that the agricultural interest has gone to the devil, and that your big landowners are merely genteel paupers.'

'Only wish I was one of you genteel paupers too,' said Anson, who was one of those extraordinary young gentlemen who had knocked about town for years, and couldn't if he tried have explained to his dearest friend how he did it; but he had one of those elastic minds that was equally prepared to discuss with his friends the raising of ten thousand pounds or a five-pound note. In fact, in his more volatile moments, he had been known to say that 'it was the insignificance of the sum required that made the difficulty. You see,' he would continue, 'when you want a few hundreds, and your name is well known about London, the money-lenders can't believe but what there is some prospect of your paying; but when you go to them for dribblets, they want to know what office you're in, or some rot of that sort. Dribblets are connected with clerkships; hundreds with visionary incomes.'

'It's a deuce of a bore,' said Lord Dartree. 'From all I hear, this is an uncommon smart colt, and the governor stands to win over a hundred thousand pounds on him. Now, if he's put up for sale, it's as likely as not that he will be bought by the very men who laid the money, under which circumstances, it is not likely he'll win the Derby next year.'

'No,' said Anson, 'it's hardly likely they'll win the race for the pleasure of paying you all this money. One don't know, but the probability is the horse will be put up for sale. Pretty sure to be, unless there is racing stock in the family; and I always understood that old Dick Bramton had neither chick nor child; never heard he had a relation of any kind. Nobody knows much about him. But he began life as a stable lad, didn't he?'

'Something of that sort,' said Lord Dartree; 'don't know exactly, but he could always win races when he meant business. The governor's no fool; and when he found out that Bramton had bought the colt he went to him at once, and said point blank, "I have got all the yearling books about Damocles for the Derby. My risk, not yours at present. You have nothing to do but to tell me at the end of his two-year-old career how much you would like of them, and you will find me quite reasonable."'

'And what did he say?' asked Anson.

'"All right, my lord,' was his reply. "If the colt turns out as good as he looks, you will have a rare run for your money."'

'It's uncertain property to invest in, a two-year-old that has never run,' remarked Anson; 'but then people wouldn't lay such liberal odds if there was not all the uncertainty about it. You'll have to buy the colt if you can, or else come to some arrangement with his new owner.'

'I suppose so,' replied Lord Dartree. 'It's a great bore. Can't understand a man like Dick Bramton getting into such a scrape. Should have thought him too clever a man to play against the tables.'

'You might have known better than that,' laughed Anson. 'Who know better the folly of backing horses than the book-makers, and yet they do it at times.'

'True,' replied Dartree; 'we all deride the idea when in London of playing against the tables, but as soon as we get to Monte Carlo we feel bound to try our luck.'

'Well, what becomes of Damocles must interest you much. Still, if any one can rise to the occasion, it is your noble father.'

'Why, that is just what I tell you he can't,' retorted Dartree irritably. 'You may know what to do, and not be able

to do it. This is a question of money,
and that is exactly what I have told you
the noble house of Ranksborow has not.'

'No,' said Anson quietly; 'but Lord
Ranksborow is a man of infinite resources,
more especially on the turf. It's very
easy to do most things with money, but
it takes a clever man to attain his ends
without. Now I have a very high
opinion of your father's talents in his own
line; indeed, in any line. Years ago, he
showed in the House of Lords what he
could do; and before that, in the House
of Commons, as Lord Dartree, was pronounced one of the most promising young
ones out. But he cut politics for racing,
and, as we all know, is as good a judge
as any man on the turf.'

'Well,' rejoined Lord Dartree, 'he has
a great opportunity now for exercising
his faculties, and by hook or by crook
acquiring the control of Damocles. Buy
the colt he can't, unless they are willing
to sell on tick, which is not at all likely.'

'No,' rejoined Anson, 'there's not much

of that in horse-dealing; still I've great confidence in your father, and only wish I had a bit of your book, for though the colt has never run, I doubt a good man laying you half the odds now.'

But if the members of the Heliotrope were fluttered at the news of the death of Dick Bramton, it made a much more considerable stir down at Newmarket. Stubber the trainer was simply, to use his own expression, 'flabbergasted.' Even his intimate friends, who really were as much puzzled and disappointed about the affair as himself, could not refrain from laughing at Mr Stubber's melancholy re-frain of 'What's to become of the hosses?' He discussed the affair with them from every point of view; he vowed that Damocles was the speediest yearling he ever tried; and look at the blood, too, by Tyrant out of Packthread; the Tyrants always stay. He eulogised the dead man, and said, 'There were few shrewder men on a racecourse than Mr Bramton. Why, he'd have won a fortune with this colt;

and now I should just like to know what's
to become of the hosses? It's cruel I've
never had the luck to train the winner
of the Derby yet, and I did think I should
do it next year.'

The curiosity to know how Dick Bramton had disposed of his property was very
great at Newmarket, but none of his
friends there seemed to be aware that he
had had a brother. In fact, though they
might be supposed to be better informed
about the dead man's family than the
members of the Heliotrope, they seemed
equally ignorant that he had either kith or
kin belonging to him. Still it is so rarely
that a man stands utterly alone in this
world, that they all supposed his property
would go to some distant relation ; but on
one point they were unanimous, and in
response to the trainer's dolorous question,
rejoined that the horses would come to the
hammer. Cold comfort all this for Sam
Stubber, who really was honestly wrapped
up in his charge. He was a conscientious
man, and thoroughly to be trusted, or he

never would have been employed by Dick
Bramton. He was a man of much experience, and though perhaps somewhat sanguine, quite understood how to try a horse.
They had very good trying tackle in the
stable, and as far as it was possible to test
a colt of the age of Damocles, Mr Staples
had done so, and with very satisfactory
results. In fact, as he told his intimates,
he had never tried a youngster so high
in his life, and the thought that his
favourite would be probably taken out
of his charge was gall and wormwood to
him; and of course it was probable that
whoever bought Damocles would transfer
the horse to his own stable. Still at
present he heard nothing from anybody
on this point, and at this Mr Stubber
and his friends marvelled greatly. What
could be the meaning of it? Could
Richard Bramton have died intestate,
and were they searching for his heir,
or had he died insolvent? He had made,
no doubt, a good bit of money on the
turf, but then there was the manner of

his death—killed in a gambling-house; and no people knew better than the Newmarket men how quickly it is possible to knock down any amount of turf winnings in houses of that description. The rooms at Newmarket, like those at Doncaster, had been wont to give instructive lessons on that point. In the meantime the spring was drawing on. The Two Thousand was a thing of the past, and the New Stakes at Ascot had been selected for the *début* of Damocles, when one morning, after returning from the Heath with his charges, Mr Stubber was informed there was a gentleman in the parlour who had arrived from London and wished to see him. Sam Stubber at once went into the room, found his visitor gazing in an absent way out of the window, and invited him to join him at breakfast.

'I shall be very glad,' replied the latter. 'The morning air gives one an appetite, and we can discuss our business over it as well as anywhere. I must at once introduce myself as Mr Pecker, of the firm of Drysdel and Pecker, solicitors. I have come down to see you about the racing stud of our late client Mr Richard Bramton.'

'Well, Mr Pecker, I'm right glad to see you, though I am afraid you bring no good news for me. What's to become of those hosses has been a sore puzzle to me. I suppose they're to be sold, and I should very much like to know who'll buy two or three of 'em.'

'Well, we've got no immediate instructions about them,' replied Mr Pecker; 'but I should suppose that would be their destiny, as far as we can guess. What I've come down here for is to make out a list of what horses there actually are, and to ask you to give me a rough valuation of them.'

'And whose property are they at this minute?' inquired Mr Stubber.

'That,' replied the attorney, ' I am not at liberty to mention, and it's possible you will never know. They will be sold as the property of the late Mr Richard Bramton ; and how he has disposed of his personal property is, I take it, of not very much consequence to anyone.'

'Before I say anything about the valuation, Mr Pecker,' rejoined the trainer, 'I should like to ask you when you think of selling these horses, because that would make a difference.'

'Oh, I see,' rejoined the lawyer, 'some times are more favourable for that sort of thing than others.'

'Just so,' replied Mr Stubber ; 'the most valuable horse, I reckon, in Mr Bramton's stud, is a two-year-old called Damocles. Now you can dispose of him, no doubt, for a good round sum by private contract ; on the other hand, you can run him for the New Stakes at Ascot in about three weeks' time—a race that he's pretty certain to win, and which, if he does win easily, will considerably increase his value.'

'And which course should you recommend, Mr Stubber ?'

'That must depend upon what sort of a man the present owner is. In the first method of disposing of the colt there is no risk, in the second there is. The youngsters in the New Stakes are mostly dark, and there may be one, though I don't think it, too good for us. If Damocles got badly beat, the gilt would be off the ginger-bread. Then there are the chances of training. Damocles is as sound as a roach, but legs will go, and hosses give trouble when least expected. If his new owner's a sportsman, he'll run him,' and Mr Stubber cast an inquiring look at the lawyer.

'I'm sure I can't say about that,' replied Mr Pecker, with an amazed look. 'I can only report what you tell me to my client. I don't understand anything about these things myself.'

'Then perhaps, sir, you wouldn't care to go round the stables?'

'On the contrary, if not against all rules, that is precisely what I should like to do,' rejoined Pecker.

'Then come along,' said Mr Stubber, 'and I'll show you Damocles, and all the rest of 'em.'

Mr Pecker was excessively pleased with all he saw, and when introduced to Damocles, a lengthy dark chesnut colt, with thighs let down like a greyhound's, not only expressed the greatest admiration for him, but was so pertinent in his remarks about his shape, that the gratified Mr Stubber, when he bade the lawyer good-bye, said,—

'Well, sir, you may know nothing about racing, but you do know a good hoss when you see one.'

CHAPTER VI.

A DELICATE COMMISSION.

'It's all very well, John, but you must exert yourself. Other folks have to do it when they go into a new neighbourhood. You must make acquaintances; people must be made to call. You've dragged us down here to Temple Rising—'

'Upon my soul, Mrs Bramton, I like that,' interrupted her husband. 'Dragged you down here, indeed, when the old villa at Wimbledon was quite good enough for me. You would have me set up as a country gentleman; you said it was more genteel. It strikes me we are not quite genteel enough for the ˋpeople round here—'

'Pooh, nonsense!' rejoined Mrs Bramton; 'they may be very great swells, but they're a poor lot. As far as I can make out, there's very few of them drive such carriages as I do. I'm sure you could buy most of them up. Even Lord Ranksborow, who has never deigned to take the slightest notion of us, I am told is as hard up as any one. You surely might scrape acquaintance with him.'

'I tell you it's impossible; it's not the thing, you know, for us to call first. I did tread upon his toe at that meeting about the flower show, and then apologise, and remark it was a fine day. I took off my hat to him quite affable the next time we met, but, Lord! he only just touched his, and evidently didn't recognise me in the slightest degree.'

'Now what did I tell you, John, were my reasons for buying a country place? Simply, I said, to get the girls well married. You've lots of money, John; now what do the girls want?—blood and position.'

'Ah! I know,' returned her husband, 'this blue blood they're always talking about; but I don't know where they sell it, or how to buy it.'

'Don't talk nonsense!' returned the lady sharply. 'There are lots of young men among these county families who would be only too glad to marry a good-looking girl with money; and, though I says it myself, my girls can bear looking at in a ballroom as well as any of them.'

'Well, it's no good talking about it, my dear. I don't see how the girls are to marry without meeting young men; and the people about here apparently don't care about knowing us. Now, when we were at Wimbledon, there were lots of—'

'John! stockbrokers and City men,' interrupted Mrs Bramton. 'Yes, I know that; but I look higher a good deal for my girls, I can tell you. We *must* make the people know us.'

'It's all very well,' replied John Bramton, 'to say we must.'

'Very well,' interposed his wife, 'then

I'll put it stronger, and say they *shall.*
You know, Mr Bramton, I'm a woman of
energy—'

'Ah! yes, my dear, and of great con-
versational powers. I have never known
you without something to say.'

And with this mild sarcasm John Bramton was about to leave the room, when
the door opened, and a footman said,—

'There's a gentleman to see you, sir,
on business.'

'What have you done with him, William ?'

'Shown him into your study, sir.'

'Quite right, William ; quite right,
William,' said Mr Bramton pompously.
'Visitors to the drawing-room, people on
business to my study,' with which remark
he followed the servant to the room in
question.

A stout, middle-aged man, with grizzled
hair, keen eyes, and a shrewd face, who
was apparently admiring the pictures on
the walls, turned abruptly and greeted
him.

'You've a beautiful place here, Mr Bramton. I couldn't help admiring it as I drove up the avenue. These pictures, too, are some of them remarkably fine.'

'Yes, I believe they are. They ought to be. I gave a lot of money for 'em. I left that department when I was furnishing to old Lazarus of Wardour Street, and he assured me they were all gems and all bargains. Ha! ha! I've been too long in business to swallow that last, Mr—' and here John Bramton paused a moment while he glanced at his visitor's card, 'Mr Skinner. Still I don't think old Lazarus would cheat me altogether.'

'I don't think Mr Bramton is a man who is easily got the best of,' replied the stranger, smiling. 'I have no doubt that you are as good a judge of a horse as you are of a picture.'

'Tol-lol,' said John Bramton, drawing himself up, and falling into his favourite attitude with his thumbs stuck into the armholes of his waistcoat. 'I keep my fellow up to the mark, I can tell you.

You'll see some rare, shiny-coated, long-tailed ones in my stables.'

'Ah,' said Mr Skinner, 'I see you know how a horse ought to look. We are a horsey nation, and there never was an Englishman who didn't consider himself a judge of a horse.'

John Bramton was flattered. The stranger had tickled him like a trout.

'A very pleasant, gentlemanly man,' thought the host; 'sees at a glance I'm a judge of pictures and horses. Whatever business he has come about doesn't seem to be urgent. I daresay he would like a walk round the grounds. Hang it! I'll ask him to lunch. We don't see many people; it'll be a change. By the way, Mr Skinner, perhaps you would like to look round the grounds?'

'Of all things,' replied the stranger.

'And will do us the favour of stopping to lunch afterwards?' continued Mr Bramton.

The stranger bowed assent, and in another minute or two they were strolling through the gardens and pleasaunce. Mr Skinner admired everything, the hothouse, the conservatory, the orchid house, vinery, and stables.

'I think Temple Rising the most perfect gentleman's seat I've ever been over, and I've had some experience. By the way, Mr Bramton, I've been so taken up in admiring the pictures, horses, flowers, etc., I quite forgot to mention that I knew your poor brother Dick very well.'

'Did you, indeed! that's odd. Poor fellow, I never knew exactly how he lived. He was always gambling. Came by his death through it.'

'It was a bad business,' said Mr Skinner; 'and how Dick Bramton came to go in for roulette, rather beats me. I suppose he found it dull out there. Nothing to do, nobody to talk racing with. He wanted a little excitement, and he would know how to take care of himself, too. I don't mean when it came to knives, for he was a little man, and a delicate man, but he was a very leading man on the turf, I assure you, Mr Bramton.'

'Ah! so I've understood lately. He left a comfortable bit of money behind him. They tell me,' and here John Bramton looked a little inquisitively at his auditor, 'that he made a regular business of it.'

Bramton, in fact, was not quite sure whether Mr Pecker had not been either mistaken himself or hoaxing him when he said that the turf could be made a business.

'Business of it! I should think he did; and so do most men who are really on it.'

'Come in at this window, Mr Skinner, and let me introduce you to the ladies, and then we'll go in to lunch.'

They stepped through the window.

'Margaret, my dear,' exclaimed John Bramton, 'let me introduce you to a friend of poor Dick's! My daughters, Mr Skinner.'

The visitor bowed, and then, turning to Mrs Bramton, said,—

'Yes, ma'am, Dick Bramton was a very old friend of mine, and was one of the cleverest men we had. No man ever made more dashing *coups* on the turf. I assure you he was well known to all the racing magnates.'

Now, Mrs Bramton, who during his lifetime had had the greatest contempt for her brother-in-law, had considerably changed her opinion since she had learnt that he had left five-and-thirty thousand pounds behind him, and left it, as she considered, though not quite properly, still satisfactorily. 'It ought to have been left,' she argued, 'to her husband in the first instance, even if it went to Dick Bramton's favourite niece afterwards.' Then she had been rather struck by the very flattering notices about him that had appeared in the papers.

'Yes,' she murmured, 'I believe he was very well known to the members of the Jockey Club.'

Mr Skinner bowed assent.

' And a very successful man besides.'

' Very,' rejoined their visitor.

' So clever, and so successful,' said Mrs Bramton, smiling sweetly, ' that I believe the Jockey Club paid him the compliment of warning him off the turf.'

Mr Skinner's sole reply was a burst of laughter; and it was a minute or two before he could at all master his risible faculties.

' Ten thousand pardons, my dear madam!' he exclaimed at length, ' but I'm sure you don't understand what you have said. "Warning off the turf" is a punishment for disgraceful practices on it; and poor Dick never did anything to warrant that extreme sentence of the Jockey Club.'

John Bramton, on hearing this explanation, exploded even more boisterously than Mr Skinner, while poor Mrs Bramton blushed as red as a peony, and Miss Bramton bit her lip with vexation, and muttered to herself,—

'Mamma is always committing some *gaucherie* like that.'

'My eye, Margaret, you have put your foot into it!' said John Bramton, as soon as he could speak. 'You see, Mr Skinner, we ain't racing people. We don't know anything about it. Poor Dick and I went different ways in life, and never saw very much of each other. When we met, you see, we had nothing in common. He didn't understand my business, nor I his. In fact, I thought his business was gambling until the other day. Now let's come in to lunch.'

'Do you live in this neighbourhood, Mr Skinner?' said Miss Bramton, as they took their places at table.

'No, I regret to say not. My business compels me to live in London; but it must be a charming part of the country. Thickly populated, so many gentlemen's places, plenty of society, and all that sort of thing.'

'Well, that's just what it isn't,' said

Mrs Bramton. 'There are plenty of people, no doubt, but they're not inclined to be sociable,—rather stiff and stand-off—'

'Mamma, mamma,' interposed Miss Bramton, 'you forget. The fact is, Mr Skinner, we are newcomers in the county, and, as you know, it always takes time to know people.'

'Yes,' said Mr Bramton, 'your ma is right, Matilda. That's just what they are, 'aughty. Now, here's my neighbour the Earl of Ranksborow, I'm sure I wish to be sociable, but he don't seem to see it.'

'I think, papa,' said Lucy quietly, 'that you're a little impatient. I daresay we shall know people in time, although not perhaps the Earl of Ranksborow.'

'I am staying at Knightshayes,' observed Mr Skinner. 'I'm sure you will find the Earl a very pleasant and courteous neighbour as soon as you know him. Somewhat quick-tempered, perhaps, but that's all.'

'Oh! no doubt,' replied John Bramton hurriedly. 'I'm sure, when I trod on his toe by accident at the flower show meeting, he accepted my apology quite affable like.'

'Well, I really must be going,' said Mr Skinner, rising. 'What with your charming place, and your kindness, I have quite forgot what I came about. I must ask for a word with you in your study before I leave.'

'Certainly,' replied Mr Bramton, and Mr Skinner having said good-bye to his hostess and her daughters, followed his entertainer to the room in question.

'The fact is,' said the visitor, 'I have been told you have inherited poor Dick Bramton's racing stud. Amongst those horses is a colt called Damocles. It has never run, but I candidly own that it is supposed to be good. I am commissioned to offer you one thousand pounds for him.'

'One thousand pounds!' ejaculated John Bramton. 'I know they give long prices for some of these racers, but a thousand pounds is a mint of money.'

'It is,' replied Mr Skinner drily. 'I have known as much paid many a time for quite as good-looking youngsters as Damocles, and they've turned out not worth a row of gingerbread.'

'Quite so, quite so,' replied John Bramton. 'A thousand pounds!—you're in earnest, Mr Skinner?'

'Never more so,' replied that gentleman. 'I'll write you a cheque for that sum now, and let you know where to send the colt after it's cashed.'

'A thousand pounds!' exclaimed John Bramton, starting to his feet. 'If poor Dick's horses sell like this, he has left a deal more than I reckoned on. Excuse me one moment, Mr Skinner,' and so saying John Bramton dashed off in search off his daughter.

'Lucy, my dear,' he exclaimed, as he pounced upon her in the drawing-room, 'here's such a chance to get rid of one of those horses. Mr Skinner has offered a thousand pounds for Dam—Dam—something.'

'Oh! papa, papa!' cried Lucy.

'No, my dear, I don't mean that. I'm not a damning anything, only I can't re-collect the name of the horse.'

'Damocles, I suppose, papa?'

'That's it. Think what a chance, Lucy; a thousand pounds for a wretched brute who does nothing but eat, and, as Mr Skinner says, may turn out good for nothing. You can buy yourself a pair of ponies, or anything you like, and put a lot into the bank besides. We shall never get such a chance again.'

'I don't know, papa; I'm not so sure about that. I know more about the value of racehorses than you do. Mr Skinner, remember, was an intimate friend of poor Uncle Dick's. The probability is, that he is a much better judge of what Damocles is worth than either of us. I know Uncle Dick thought a great deal of that horse; besides, what made Mr Skinner come all the way from London to offer you a thousand pounds for that horse, if he didn't think he was going to make a good bargain ?'

'Pooh! he didn't come down on purpose. He's staying,' continued Mr Bramton pompously, and sticking his thumbs into the armholes of his waistcoat, ' with my neighbour, The Right Honourable the Earl of Ranksborow.'

'Well, never mind where he came from, papa. He wouldn't come over here quietly and offer you a thousand pounds if he didn't think he was getting Damocles cheaply.'

' Upon my word, Lucy, I believe you're right. You see I never dealt in these kind of goods before. Perhaps that Skinner is trying to " best " me. Never mind, Lucy, you'll find your old father is a match for most of them,' and so saying John Bramton returned to the study.

'Well, Mr Skinner,' he said, as he entered, ' I don't think it'll quite do. My girls have a fancy for that horse. I think it 'ud make a nice lady's 'orse, for instance.'

Mr Skinner opened his eyes wide. That a man should go and consult his wife and daughters about the disposal of a racehorse was to him a thing past all understanding. Recovering himself, with an easy smile, he said,—

'You will have your joke, Mr Bramton. Not quite enough, eh? Well, I'll make it guineas.'

But all John Bramton's business instincts were now thoroughly awakened. If Mr Skinner could afford to spring in his bidding, it was obvious that he was offering considerably less than the valuation he put upon the colt in question.

'No,' said John Bramton; 'I won't sell him just at present.'

'Well, no harm done,' replied Mr Skinner, as he rose to go. 'I have had the pleasure of making your acquaintance, and shall be able to tell Lord Ranksborow what very charming neighbours he has got.'

'Ah! do now, do now. That's kindly of you. Tell him we do the thing tollolish. Very glad if his lordship will come in and take a snack with us any time he is passing this way.'

Mr Bramton insisted upon accompanying his guest to the door, where a neat dogcart was awaiting him. Just before stepping into it, Mr Skinner turned and said,—

'I tell you what, it's overstepping my commission, but I'll take my chance of that. This is my last word. Here's twelve hundred for Damocles, and I'll write you a cheque this minute.'

'No, no, thank ye,' replied Mr Bramton. 'No; you see we've taken a fancy to the horse—quite a pet in the family— not to be thought of. Good-bye, good-bye; so glad to have seen you. Remember me to his lordship,' and with these words Mr Bramton bustled back into the house.

'Good Lord!' he muttered, 'to think that I should ever refuse twelve hundred pounds for a horse. If he had button-holed me a minute longer on the steps, I must have taken it. Oh, dear! if Lucy is wrong, I shall never forgive myself for having missed a chance like that.'

CHAPTER VII.

MR SKINNER REPORTS PROGRESS.

THE Right Honourable the Earl of Ranksborow had been not at all badly described by Anson at the Heliotrope— an undoubtedly clever man, a brilliant man in pretty nearly everything he essayed, but wanting in one great thing, namely, stability of purpose. He was always disappointing his friends in whatever pursuit he took up. His early efforts were invariably so crowned with success that great things were expected of him. At one time in the political world he was regarded as one of the most rising young men of his party. He was then Lord Dartree ; and it was prophesied of him that, with practice, he would become one of the best speakers in the House. But suddenly he cast politics on one side and took to steeple-chasing, and distinguished himself at first by riding with great dash but equal want of judgment. However, he threw himself into his new pursuit with all the ardour habitual to him, and racing men were soon full of astonishment at the way in which he improved. At one time he had dabbled in literature, and some of his hunting and society ballads were in all the world's mouth. One thing after another he took up only to throw upon one side just as he was beginning to make a name in it. As one of his most intimate friends said at the time, ' Dartree is a rare beginner, but he can't stay.' To all the pursuits of his youth the Earl had remained faithful only to the turf and the whist-table. He had lost thousands at the former, but the latter was no doubt worth some hundreds a year to him. He was a scientific player, and nobody had ever seen the Earl lose his head either on the race-course or at the card-table, which, considering his naturally hot temper, showed that he had considerable strength of mind when his interests required it.

'So you bungled it, Skinner. I gave you a pretty liberal limit, too; and, from all I can hear, this John Bramton was neither likely to want the colt nor to be aware of his value.'

'No, my lord,' rejoined Skinner quietly, 'I have made no mess of it whatever. I did not bid to anything like what you said I might. It would have been no good; it would have been showing one's hand for nothing. This John Bramton knows nothing of horses, but is a shrewd man, with commercial instincts. The minute he found I wanted the colt, he rushed at the conclusion that it was worth more than I bid for it. He doesn't know what it's worth, but he is terribly afraid of letting it go under its full value.'

'And there are plenty of people to tell him that,' growled the Earl.

'Yes,' rejoined Skinner; 'and you know, my lord, there are plenty of people would go a good deal higher for the colt than you authorised me.'

'Yes! Confound it! I'd bid high enough if I had it, but then I haven't. Damocles is worth more to me than he is to any one else.'

The scene of the above conversation was Lord Ranksborow's private den at Knightshayes—a very different sanctum from that of Mr Bramton. Instead of pictures, the walls were lined with book-cases containing a curious medley of literature. The *Racing Calendar* stood cheek by jowl with Horace, Juvenal, Tacitus, etc., while the English classics were mixed up with the *Sporting Magazine* and numerous old books which referred to the turf in its earlier days. Above the fireplace was a large oil-painting—the sole one in the room—representing the great match between Voltigeur and the Flying

Dutchman, run over the Knavesmire in '52, while opposite this was a tall mahogany cabinet with glass doors, through which you could see trays filled with cigars of every description, something like one of those cabinets in which collectors keep birds' eggs, only on a larger scale.

Mr Skinner had so far told the truth when he had said that he was staying at Knightshayes. Indeed he often came down for a night or two; but he certainly had not informed Mr Bramton of his exact position there. He was a very leading turf commissioner, and amongst his clients had for many years numbered Lord Ranksborow. In fact, in the early part of his career, Mr Skinner had been indebted to the Earl for many remunerative commissions, and owed his first start in his vocation to that nobleman having taken him up and recommended him to two or three of his racing friends. But the Earl treated him completely as a man of business. He was always comfortably put up, an excellent dinner and bottle

of wine was always provided for him, and
Lord Ranksborow would sometimes dine
with him in the library ; but, he would
have as soon thought of asking his butler
to join the family circle as Mr Skinner.

'What the deuce is to be done ? I
fancied the looks of that colt immensely
when he came into the sale-ring. When
Dick Bramton endorsed my judgment
by giving a long sum for him, I fancied
him still more, and, as you know, I
snapped every yearling book I could get
hold of about him. Of course I told Dick
he could have as much as he wanted, and
he told me, poor fellow, just before he
went to Egypt, that he had tried him—"a
clipper." Stubber told me the same thing
again this spring. I never had such a
chance ; and now, goodness knows into
whose hands the colt will go. What the
devil is to be done, Skinner ? Take a
weed, Skinner. Put on your considering
cap, and think it out,' and as he spoke
the Earl pushed his cigar-box across to
his commissioner.

The latter carefully selected a Cabana from the box, lit it, and smoked for two or three minutes in silence.

' There's only one way out of it that I can see, my lord,' he observed at length.

' I suppose you mean a big ten thousand pounds and have done with it. I tell you I can't; I haven't got it.'

' No; I don't mean that exactly. I think I see a way by which you might possibly become owner of Damocles for very much less money than that; say for the fifteen hundred which you author-ised me to go to. And you know, my lord, that anybody who knew anything about horse-flesh would simply laugh at such a bid as that. Our only chance of getting hold of Damocles was Mr Bram-ton's total ignorance of everything con-nected with racing.'

' All's fair in horse-dealing,' rejoined the Earl sharply. ' Be good enough, Skinner, to remember that I don't employ you to moralise, but to act.'

His lordship was quite aware that, in

attempting to buy Damocles at the figure he proposed, he was being guilty of a piece of uncommon sharp practice, and by no means relished being reminded of it by his subordinate.

'Well, my lord,' said Skinner, 'I think if you would drive over to Temple Rising and see Mr Bramton yourself, and offer him the fifteen hundred, he would very likely take it from you.'

'I don't see that he is more likely to take the price from one man than another. If you thought that, why the deuce didn't you offer it him?'

'Because, my lord, I don't want to lose your custom. I've heard you say again and again that you never employ fools knowingly. I purposely stopped at twelve hundred, in order to leave you an opening.'

'I'll be hung if I understand you!' exclaimed the Earl.

'Mr Bramton has just bought a property near you, and is simply dying to make your acquaintance. Take my advice ; call upon him at once, admire his place and welcome him cordially to the country. Call upon him again two or three days later, offer him fifteen hundred for Damocles, and I'll bet you a level fiver it's a deal.'

'What! call upon that d—d trades-man!' exclaimed the Earl.

'Think of Damocles,' softly murmured Mr Skinner, and then Lord Ranksborow burst into a peal of laughter.

'What on earth put this idea into your head ?'

'When one goes horse-dealing, one naturally looks out for the weak points both of the horse and his owner. You know the old cant, my lord, of the dealer's yard, " I wouldn't part with that animal to any one but a real horseman like yourself." Of course the dealer there is simply tick-ling his customer's vanity. You must tickle Mr Bramton's vanity. I don't sup-pose he ever knew a real lord before, and he's just simply death upon knowing one now.'

'By Jove! I'll do it, Skinner!' cried the peer, laughing, 'I'll do it!'

'Remember, the sooner the better. As soon as it oozes out who Damocles belongs to, it's quite likely there will be others as anxious to buy as we are.'

'Yes, and with more money,' muttered the Earl. 'No, you're quite right; it must be done at once. I'll drive over to-morrow afternoon.'

'By the way,' said Skinner, laughing, 'I quite forgot Bramton's message. He sent you his kind regards, and he hoped, any time you were passing, you would drop in and take a snack.'

'Confound his impudence!' exclaimed the Earl.

'He further bid me tell you,' continued Skinner, his mouth twitching with sup-pressed laughter, 'that they did the thing tol-lolish at Temple Rising.'

For a moment Lord Ranksborow's eyes flashed, and then the absurdity of the whole thing struck him, and he once more burst out into a peal of laughter.

'I will, Skinner; by heavens, I will! On the strength of that message, I'll go over to lunch there to-morrow. I'll make myself deuced agreeable both to Bramton and all the ladies of the family.'

'There's one thing more, my lord. Do you think the ladies of your family—'

'Stop, sir,' interrupted the Earl. 'My calling is one thing; it does not much matter whom I know. With the Countess and my daughters it's a very different thing.'

'Well, my lord, of course it's not for me even to pretend to know anything about these things, but remember it's a card in your hand. If the Countess would call, and you could just once in a way ask them over to a family dinner, upon my word, when you came to the wine and walnuts, I think Mr Bramton would *give* you Damocles.'

'You mean well, Skinner, but I can't have the Countess and my daughters mixed up with such a menagerie as this.'

'I can be of no further use to you, my

lord, in this matter, and will be off by the early train to-morrow morning. Any other instructions you have got to give me, you will of course write or wire to the Victoria Club.'

' Good-night, Skinner ; you've done your best, and though you couldn't accomplish the deal, we have at all events got soundings.'

' Good-night, my lord,' rejoined the commissioner, as he threw the end of his cigar into the fireplace and took his bedroom candle.

'A shrewd fellow that,' muttered the Earl, as the door closed behind his agent. ' I always said he would come to the top of the tree ; and I suppose he has the working of quite half the big commissions that come into the market, and nobody understands the manipulation of the strings about a big handicap better. That was a masterly stroke of his, stopping at twelve hundred ! It leaves me the chance of offering fifteen hundred in an outburst of patrician liberality,' and the Earl chuckled at his own sarcasm. 'What a judge of human nature the beggar is! He turned that John Bramton inside out during the couple of hours he spent at Temple Rising. Poor Molyneux! to think that Temple Rising should pass into the hands of a fellow who has made his money in soap boiling, grey shirtings, or some such business. It seems but yesterday Molyneux and I had our cottage at Newmarket, and always took a place at Ascot together. I wonder where he is now. I implored him to hedge his Vanguard money that Cesarewitch day, and I can recollect now the smile with which he said, "It's neck or nothing this time, old man. I've got every acre of Temple Rising on it. I'm going for the gloves, and intend to be a man or a mouse over this," and mouse it was. Ah, well, if Knightshayes hadn't been strictly entailed, I'm not certain it would be in the family now. Well, to-morrow I must go over and call upon this vulgar tradesman, I suppose. If I could only get Damocles into my own hands, I'd give the ring a shaker. Sharp fellow, Skinner, and not given to make mistakes. I hope he hasn't made one upon this occasion. By the way, I wonder what Skinner was. He must have had a superior education and bringing up, he is so much better mannered than most of his brethren. An odd thing one is always hearing stories of what the leading bookmakers were before they took to their present profession. Heaven knows whether these legends are true or not, but the odd thing is I never heard anybody claim to know what Skinner's antecedents might have been,' and absorbed in this conjecture, his lordship betook himself to his chamber.

As for the subject of these speculations, he murmured, as he laid his head upon his pillow,—

'He'll only half do it, I know. His confounded pride will stand in his way. Yet, if any man on the turf wants a turn, it's the Earl of Ranksborow. If he would only just put his pride in his pocket, drive over to Temple Rising with the Countess, and be a bit sociable with the Bramtons, he might just now have Damocles at his own price. I'll lay a hundred but he'll only half do it to start with, and before he has thoroughly made up his mind to swallow the Bramtons, John Bramton will have come at the fact that the colt is worth a deal of money.

CHAPTER VIII.

LORD RANKSBOROW CALLS.

JOHN BRAMTON's daughters had been, as is so often the case, brought up in a very different style from their father and mother. They were quite ignorant of the genteel poverty in which their parents' early days had been passed. They had never seen anything of that close economy in the household which had been necessary, when they were too young to recollect it, in order to make both ends meet. John Bramton had got his foot upon the ladder when he ventured to marry, and his progress up it had been rapid.

By the time Matilda and Lucy Bramton

were children old enough to take note of such things, their father, though not rich, was in comfortable circumstances, and from that time his store increased rapidly year by year. He was a capital business man, and a lucky one to boot, as lucky in one line as his brother had been in another. His daughters were sent to the best of schools, and finished off at a fashionable boarding-school. They were pretty, lady-like girls, but differed a good deal in disposition. Matilda was burning with a desire to push her way into good society, and looked down upon her father's old friends and acquaintances with the greatest contempt. She it was who, working through her mother, had been the main cause of their selling the villa at Wimbledon and purchasing the estate of Temple Rising from its luckless and ruined owner. She wished to sever all connection with what she was pleased to term her father's ' City set,' and had only just discovered that it does not follow that, because you settle in a

county, that county will receive you with
open arms.

Lucy differed in some respects from her
sister. She was quite as much awake to
the pleasures of good society as Matilda.
It was natural that both girls, refined as
they had been by their bringing up, should
shrink a little from the boisterous jokes
and vulgarity of their father's old friends.
He himself often set Matilda's teeth on
edge in this wise; and of her mother's
gaucheries that young lady had much
horror. Lucy was equally alive to her
parents' weaknesses in this wise; but the
difference between the two girls was this:
that whereas Matilda could scarcely conceal her impatience of her father and
mother's failings, Lucy never forgot that
they were her father and mother—a cir-
cumstance which, when irritated, Matilda,
if she remembered, was apt to take slight
heed of.

The Miss Bramtons, in short, had been
educated to a standard considerably above
that in which their parents habitually

mixed, and it was little wonder that they were both somewhat discontented with their lot. It is hard upon girls who have been brought up as ladies, to be unable to find amongst the men of their acquaintance any whom they can quite regard as gentlemen, and that was one reason that made Lucy so fond of travelling about with her late uncle.

Dick Bramton, although by no means a refined man, was not so essentially vulgar as his brother. If he mixed on the turf with a rough lot, he also associated there with men of undeniable polish and culture, such as the Earl of Ranksborow, to wit. Then, while travelling with him, Lucy came across many pleasant people, who were also wandering, and who, whatever they might be at home, were unmistakably well-bred. A pretty girl like Lucy Bramton was almost sure to attract the best young men, either on the steamers or at the *table d'hôte*, to her side ; and she found their society infinitely more pleasant than that of those young gentlemen in business who frequented the villa at Wimbledon.

It would be absurd to suppose that Lucy had forgotten that tall, good-looking dragoon whom she had met at Shepheard's Hotel. Captain Cuxwold had stood as far as he could between her and the first great sorrow of her life. She had been inexpressibly shocked and grieved at her uncle's death—an uncle who, let his faults be whatever they might, had always been most kind and indulgent to her. Cuxwold, she knew, had saved her an infinity of trouble, and she felt very grateful to him, not only for the trouble he had taken, but also for the delicate consideration he had shown in all the arrangements he had made for her. It was natural, under these circumstances, that he should be often present to her thoughts. Moreover, the war clouds were once more rolling up over the desert, and whether the Government liked it or not, whether they cared to save Khartoum, or whether they did not, it was evident to all men that the Mahdi had to

be confronted and stemmed. From the
sands of the desert, from the waters of the
Oxus and Zaxartes, there has never been
any difficulty about gathering a horde of
warlike adventurers whenever a leader
arose who, dubbing himself prophet, fired
the fanaticism of his followers, and filled
their souls with the lust of plunder. From
time immemorial the bait dangled before
the eyes of the Turcoman has been India;
and again and again has he swept through
the wild Afghan country, and spread deso-
lation to the banks of the Ganges. To
the Arab, the lure has always been Lower
Egypt; and when the green banner of the
prophet was first unfurled, it seemed as
if little less than the domination of all
Europe would content the wild horsemen
of the desert.

Little use to say the Mahdi was a mere
fakir, an outcast priest come from the
scum of the people, what you will. He
was a force and a focus for thousands of
the wild hordes of the desert; and un-
disciplined though they might be, these

children of the sandy sea were men of
thews and sinews, reckless of life, and
could be depended upon to follow their
chiefs to the death. Interest began to
rise high in England when the fact was
grasped that the roar of public indignation
had at last made the Government tardily
decide to rescue the man whom they had
sent to pacify the Soudan, and then apparently forgotten.   There was something
dramatic in the picture of this one man
breasting the full flood of fanaticism ; in
this leader, abandoned by his chiefs, standing with colossal heroism in the breach
against anarchy ; in this one man dominat-
ing, by sheer ascendancy of will, over the
half-hearted and treacherous population of
a city, and inducing them to stand the
privations of a siege. The attention of
England was centred on the hero of Khartoum, and the problem now was by what
means could assistance be most speedily
conveyed to him ; and over this point
there was much discussion amongst the
great military chiefs of the kingdom.

That the expedition would have no easy task before it was perfectly well recognised, and that the race they were about to encounter were made of very different stuff from the Egyptians they so easily beat at Tel-el-Kebir, was also perfectly well known.

From having been in Egypt, and heard a great deal of course about the first campaign, Lucy naturally took a very deep interest in everything connected with the country. More especially did she feel interested as to what share the 24th Lancers might bear in the forthcoming expedition.

She had promised Captain Cuxwold at parting to let him know of her safe arrival in England. That promise had been duly kept, and she had received in reply a very pleasant, chatty letter, in which the writer, while expressing himself intensely sick of Cairo, wound up by saying,—' But there surely must be work for some of us before long. The whole world will cry shame on England if she abandon Gordon at

Khartoum, though how we are to get to him, I confess I don't see. However, thank Heaven, that's a point which our chiefs have to determine; but it is not likely that the Arabs will allow us to promenade the desert without trying what we're made of.' And then, congratulating her upon being in England instead of grilling at Cairo, he concluded with 'Most sincerely yours, Jack Cuxwold.'

We are all apt, on the verge of a campaign, to speculate whether our friends, relations, or even acquaintances will take part in it, and therefore it is small wonder that Lucy Bramton constantly wondered whether the 24th Lancers would take part in this expedition, which the papers foretold was not likely to attain its end without some sharp fighting of the tribes of the desert.

Mr Bramton was sitting in the drawing-room, yawning over the *Times*, and, sooth to say, not a little weary of his new *rôle* of a country gentleman.

'It's all very well, Margaret,' he observed, 'but I like Wimbledon better.
There were always lots of people to come
and see us. at Wimbledon, and then I
could always run into the City, and have
a crack with my old friends. No; I
know, my dear, this is very genteel, but
it's devilish dull.'

'Nonsense! You'll be all right when
we get to know people, and when you've
been made a magistrate. You ought to
farm a bit; it's the proper thing for a
country gentleman to do.'

'Is it? Then for once, Mrs Bramton,
I decline to play the part of a country
gentleman. Farming means ruin to those
who understand it. What it means to
those who don't, I'm sure I can't guess.
Oh, dear! I wish lunch was ready; it's
something to do, at all events.'

Suddenly the door was thrown open,
not by a footman, but by the butler in
person, who in full unctuous tones rolled
out the name of 'The Earl of Ranksborow.' The announcement of their

noble neighbour fell like a bombshell upon the worthy pair. Mrs Bramton at once began to shake out her skirts, while as for her husband, he bounced out of his chair, and advancing to the Earl, who was making his way up the room, exclaimed,—

'How d'ye do, my lord? Happy to make your lordship's acquaintance. Lovely day, isn't it?'

'How d'ye do, Mrs Bramton?' said the Earl, as, having shaken hands with his host, he crossed to address the lady of the house. 'I got a message from an acquaintance of mine whom you were good enough to show your place to yesterday; and I've taken you at your word you see, Mr Bramton. I was passing, and I've come in to beg some lunch.'

'Only too happy, my lord,' rejoined Bramton, as he made a nervous snatch at the bell. 'Lunch, Peters, at once,' he remarked to the butler, as that functionary entered the room ; 'and Peters, ahem !'

and here the little man indulged in a perfect code of telegraphic signals, and finally grievously tried Lord Ranksborow's gravity by exclaiming, in a most audible stage whisper, ' the extra dry, remember, Peters.'

' He evidently means doing me tol-lolish,' thought the Earl, struggling hard to restrain his laughter.

' It's a beautiful place your husband has bought, Mrs Bramton. Temple Rising always puts me out of all conceit with Knightshayes. My place is bigger, but it's not half so pretty as this ; nor is my old barrack near so comfortable a house as yours.'

' You know it well, of course, my lord ? ' said Mrs Bramton.

' Known it all my life,' replied the Earl. ' Poor Molyneux was a great friend of mine, and, without the slightest disparagement to you, I own I was very sorry to lose him as a neighbour. However, we must all bow to the inevitable ; and I can only hope I shall be on as good terms with his successors as I was with himself.'

Oh! Lord Ranksborow, Lord Ranksborow! Damocles once yours, and it's little you will trouble your head about the newcomers at Temple Rising.

At this moment the two Miss Bramtons entered, and the Earl was most decidedly astonished.

'Two deuced pretty, ladylike girls,' he muttered to himself. 'Who the deuce would ever have thought that a couple of vulgarians like these could have reared two such thoroughbred-looking chicks as those!'

He advanced and shook hands with the young ladies most cordially, welcomed them heartily to the county, and congratulated them upon being the possessors of the prettiest place in it.

'You're laughing at us, Lord Ranksborow,' said Miss Bramton, smiling. 'I fancy we dwindle into insignificance by the side of Knightshayes.'

'That, I trust, you will soon have an

opportunity of judging for yourself. As
I was telling Mr Bramton just now, my
place may be bigger, but yours has it
altogether in point of beauty.'

All through luncheon the Earl won
golden opinions on all sides. He talked,
perhaps, chiefly to Miss Matilda, but he
was far too experienced a man of the
world not to, as far as possible, make
the conversation general. Mrs Bramton,
however, could be persuaded to take but
little part in it. She was somewhat
awestruck by her guest, and still more
was she afraid of committing herself and
being pounced upon by her eldest daughter. Miss Matilda snubbed her mother
rather sharply at times for the solecisms
she was wont to commit. The meal
over, the Earl wished the ladies good-
bye, and said airily,—

'I'll just have a weed in your sanctum,
Bramton, before I start.'

'Certainly, my lord, certainly,' was the
reply, and that gentleman led the way
to his own room at once.

Once seated there, and his cigar comfortably alight, Lord Ranksborow proceeded at once to business.

'Your brother was an old friend of mine,' he said; 'and I hear he has left you all his horses?'

'Well, in a way, so to speak,' replied John Bramton.

'You're not much of a racing man, I think,' continued the Earl, 'or else I must have heard of you before. If it's a fair question, what do you think of doing with them? Will they be for sale?'

'Damocles, Damocles,' muttered Mr Bramton to himself; 'dash my wig, if he ain't after Damocles! Lucy has got some gumption in her; that horse is worth a lot of money. I know he's worth twelve hundred pounds, because I refused that sum for him yesterday.'

'I'm sure I don't know, my lord. I don't know much about such things myself. I don't suppose poor Dick's nags are of much account.'

'The old fox,' thought the Earl, 'is

not quite such an innocent as Skinner pronounced him. Yesterday told him that one of them, at all events, was worth money.'

'Ah, well, if they are to come to the hammer, I should like to know. There's one or two of them I should like to have. Indeed, if you think of selling them by private contract, shall be very glad to have the refusal of them.'

'Well, my lord, I haven't at all made up my mind as yet.'

'You've a young one called Damocles,' continued the peer, as he flipped the ash off his cigar. 'Now, I can give you a good round sum for him, if you like to part with him. Now, I'm not going to beat about the bush, or have any shilly-shally about it—that's all very well amongst horse-copers, but it's not the thing between gentlemen. Now, once for all, Bramton, I've taken a fancy to Damocles. Will fifteen hundred pounds buy him? If not, there's no more to be said.'

'Fifteen hundred? That's a deal of money, to say nothing of the opportunity of obliging your lordship. Excuse me for one moment, I'll just go and consult —that is to say, I'll just go and look at some papers. I should just like to mention it. Poor Dick's last will and testament, you know.'

'Now, what in Heaven's name does he mean by all that farrago? He surely can't mean to consult Mrs Bramton about selling a horse. I wonder if he'll bite? By Jove! what a *coup* if he does.'

A few minutes and Mr Bramton re-enters the room.

'I'm very sorry, my lord, awfully sorry,' he exclaimed, 'but I can't give you any decided answer to-day! I won't say no, but I can't say yes.'

'All right,' said the Earl, 'no harm done. Send me a line over to Knight-shayes when you've made up your mind. Good-bye; very glad to have made your acquaintance,' and with these words the Earl took his departure.

' There now,' said Mr Bramton, ' Lucy
has done it. Fifteen hundred for a horse
—the friendship of an earl—a first-class
introduction to all the county, and dam'me
if the girl hasn't said no to it.'

CHAPTER IX.

No man could be more profoundly ignorant of racing matters than Mr Bramton. He would as soon have thought of reading Horace in the original as the sporting intelligence in the newspapers, and would have understood as much about the one as the other; but John Bramton's trading instincts were much too quick not to see that Damocles was a very valuable colt. What the horse might be worth he had no conception, but he had not been buying and selling all his life not to feel perfectly sure that neither Mr Skinner nor Lord Ranksborow had bid him full value. About the declining of Mr

Skinner's offer, he had no doubt but that
Lucy had persuaded him to do rightly;
but the Earl's was quite another matter.
He felt pretty sure that the fifteen
hundred was considerably less than the
colt ought to fetch; but then there was
the contingency. Fifteen hundred pounds
and the friendship of the Ranksborow
family! Surely it was worth while to let
the Earl have a bargain, and by that
means arrive at intimacy with him and
his. Mr Bramton ought to have known
better than to believe that laying a man
under an obligation can be relied on to
entail his gratitude and friendship. He
had been angry and dumbfoundered at
Lucy's refusal to at once conclude the sale
of Damocles, but there was no time to
argue the matter out then, as the Earl was
awaiting his decision. There was nothing
for it but to temporise, so having briefly
informed his daughter that she was a
headstrong little fool, he rushed back to
his own room, and gave Lord Ranksborow the undecided answer we know of.

Lucy was destined to have a somewhat uncomfortable time of it for the next two days. Her whole family were up in arms against her. In the eyes of her mother and sister, Lord Ranksborow's offer had been princely; and then it was so unkind, so ill-tempered of her, to throw obstacles in the way of their entering county society. Such an opening as this might never occur again; and, when the Earl was so anxious to be friendly, it was so ungracious not to part with a horse she had never seen and could not possibly want.

'This Damocles—such a name to give a horse!' cries Miss Matilda—'is of no use except for racing purposes; and though ladies go racing, yet nobody ever heard of their owning racehorses!'

An observation which once more endorses the correctness of Mr Biglow's famous line, 'That they didn't know everything down in Judee.'

But Lucy was obstinate. She said first of all it was by no means clear that they had a right to dispose of these horses until the engagements they were entered for were over ; but, supposing that she had the legal right, her uncle had left her everything, had been very kind to her all his lifetime, and she thought she owed it to his memory to carry out his last wishes as far as she could. She reminded them all that his dying message to her had been to 'take care of Damocles ;' then again she argued,—

'Remember what we've heard about the Earl of Ranksborow since we've been here. We know very well that, though he is a nobleman with a large estate, he is a notoriously hard-up man. Nobody suggests for one moment that he is narrow or illiberal in his dealings ; it is simply that he has a great deal to keep up, and barely the money to do it with. Is it likely, father, that he could afford to make you a fair bid for a horse ?'

'As a business man, Lucy, I tell you fairly I think you're probably right ; but this horse is nothing to you, and just

think what it means to us all. Why, it'll
lead to you and Matilda making the
acquaintance of all the surrounding nobility and gentry.'

But Lucy stuck to her guns, and positively refused to give her consent to the
acceptance of Lord Ranksborow's offer,
upon which her father angrily reminded
her that she was a minor, and that, as
her trustee, he should act as he thought
best for her, and take the earliest opportunity of disposing of such a very tick-
lish property as a stud of racehorses.

How far Mr Bramton would have proceeded to carry out his threat is proble-
matical, but the second day brought help
to Lucy from a very unexpected quarter.
Mr Bramton was proudly contemplating
his domain from the terrace outside the
drawing-room window, when a footman
came to him and said,—

'A gentleman to see you, sir, on business. Hasn't got a card, sir, but gives
the name of Stubber.' ·

'Stubber, Stubber,' said Mr Bramton

meditatively; 'never heard the name in my life. What have you done with him, William?'

'Shown him into your private room, sir.'

'Quite right,' said Mr Bramton. 'Now I wonder what this fellow can want?' and so saying, he trotted off to discover.

Stubber was a trainer of the old school. A slight, wiry, keen-eyed man of fifty or thereabouts, attired in a broad-skirted, pepper-and-salt coat, drab breeches and gaiters. He rose from his chair as Mr Bramton entered the room, and said,—

'Morning, sir; I'd have been down to pay my respects before, only I didn't know who the horses belonged to. I'm told Mr Richard has left the whole string to you?'

'Another of them, by gum! He's come about Damocles,' muttered John Bramton to himself. 'I wonder whether he wants to buy him? Not likely I'm going to part with that valuable animal to a fellow like him when there's an earl

wanting to buy him. Well, yes,' he
replied at length, 'that's about the size
of it.'

'Well, sir, I always gave your poor
brother every satisfaction, and, though I
ses it myself, I know my business, and
can pitch 'em out as fit as any man in
England.'

'Quite so, my good man,' replied John
Bramton, 'though what you propose to
pitch out, and what your business may
be, I'm blessed if I've the slightest idea.'

'Why, sir, I'm poor Mr Richard's
trainer. I've come down to talk to you
about them hosses; and I do hope you'll
leave 'em with me.'

'Ah!' rejoined Mr Bramton, with a
long-drawn breath of a man who suddenly
makes a startling discovery, 'you're the
keeper of Damocles? I mean, that you've
charge of that valuable animal. Keeper,
no; that's what they say of the people
in charge of the wild beasts in the Zoolo-
gical Gardens. You're the—what was it
you called yourself?'

'Trainer, sir. I've trained for Mr Richard for the last eight years ; and as for Damocles, he's a clinker, he is. I don't think I ever had such a colt in my charge before.'

'Ah!' said Mr Bramton patronisingly, and speaking as if he had been in the habit of winning the Derby every four or five years for some time past, 'I'm told he's a nice 'orse. Why, I was bid fifteen hundred pounds for him the beginning of the week.'

'Fifteen hundred pounds!' ejaculated the trainer, in tones of the most profound contempt.

'Just so, just so,' continued Mr Bramton. 'I thought it wasn't enough. Now, Mr Stubber, what do you consider the value of a "clinker?"'

'Damocles is well worth five thousand pounds this very minute, and will be well worth ten before a fortnight is over our heads.'

John Bramton was thunderstruck. He had been quite prepared to urge his daughter to sacrifice a little money with a view to getting the entrance into the county society they wished. He would have said, and with some reason, to Lucy, 'You're a rich young woman, and it is well worth your while to sacrifice two or three hundred pounds in order to gain a good social position.' But he had made his own money much too hardly to think of throwing away thousands for any such shadowy idea as that. No man more likely to have said, 'The money will stick to you, my girl, and society perhaps won't.'

'Why do you say, Mr Stubber,' he said, at length, 'that this horse will be worth so much more in a fortnight?'

'Well, sir,' replied the trainer, 'there is no certainty in racing, but I'm as confident as a man can be about anything connected with it, that Damocles will win the New Stakes at Ascot the week after next, and, I think, easily too. If he does, I can only say, in my opinion, considering how heavily he is engaged, he'll be worth double the money he is now. Whatever else you may sell, sir, I do hope you won't sell him, and I further venture to hope you'll leave him in my charge. Be guided by me, sir ; don't part with him, at all events till after Ascot ; and if you're not satisfied with the way he runs, then say Sam Stubber is an old fool, and isn't fit to look after a horse.'

'Well, Mr Stubber,' said Bramton, 'I promise you, at all events, the horses shall be left with you till after Ascot, and by that time I shall probably have made up my mind what to do about them.'

'Thank'ee, sir. Maybe you'll come down and look at the horses? I should like you to see Damocles have his wind up before Ascot.'

'Thank you,' said Mr Bramton. 'I don't know much about such things myself. Don't quite understand how you wind a horse up either, but I suppose, like clocks, it's a mistake to overdo it.'

The trainer smiled as he replied,—

'Too bad of you, Mr Bramton, to gammon me in this way, and pretend you know nothing about racing. That's just where it is, many a good stake is thrown away by over-winding.'

'It strikes me I'm getting on in this new line of business,' thought Mr Bramton. 'No,' he said, 'Stubber, I don't understand it, and I shall leave you to manage matters for yourself, at all events till after Ascot.'

'Very well, sir,' replied the trainer. 'If you do change your mind, there's my address, and I can give you a comfortable bedroom, and a decent dinner; but now I will say good-bye. I suppose you would like the result of the New Stakes telegraphed?'

'Yes, I think so, Stubber. I'm not much of a race-goer myself. Good-bye.'

Mr Bramton sat for some time lost in thought after the trainer had departed. It was quite obvious to him that his noble friend the Earl of Ranksborow had endeavoured to drive an uncommonly good bargain for himself, if from no

other point of view than that of buying
a thing to-day to sell for two or three
times the sum to-morrow. Then it suddenly flashed across him that Mr Skinner
was staying at Knightshayes. Of course
they were in collusion. What a fool
he had been; they had striven to buy
Damocles for about a fourth of his value.
John Bramton might know nothing about
racing, but his business instincts were
very wide awake to buying cheap and
selling dear, and that the Earl and his
confederate saw their way into that he
made no doubt.

'Well,' he muttered to himself, 'folks
who have tried to best John Bramton
have generally got the worst of it. His
lordship has tried to "do" me, and, in
my way, I'll just see if I can't "do" his
lordship. He wants something out of
me; I want something out of him. A
regular game at cribbage between us;
but his lordship will find that I can lay
out for my crib quite as cleverly as he
can,' and Mr Bramton quite chuckled at

the game he was about to play with Lord Ranksborow.'

The first thing he did was to indite a diplomatic letter to the Earl, which, it was rather fortunate for him, did not fall under the eyes of his wife or daughters. He was dreadfully given, on these occasions, to drop into the idioms of his own business, and though somewhat suspicious of what a shrewd correspondent he was dealing with, the peer could not but laugh at some of the expressions in the letter.

' I'm sorry I cannot yet give your lordship a definite answer about your offer for Damocles, but the fact I have got to consider is whether the goods, that is horses, will not sell better wholesale than by dropping into the retail business. In the event of the latter, your lordship may depend upon having the very first offer of the colt you are anxious to secure.'

Lord Ranksborow laughed when he got this letter, but he was not in the least deceived by it. He was quite as astute a man in his own way as the master of Temple Rising.

'Skinner, my friend,' he muttered, 'you made a great mistake when you thought this man was a fool. He's as sharp as a needle; he has already found out that these horses are valuable, how valuable he don't know, but he is not going to sell them until he does. That he is very anxious to make my acquaintance, and be asked, with his wife and daughters, to Knightshayes is equally clear. Well, we are not in the habit of selling our hospitality, and that's a very ugly name to give the transaction, but for all that, Mr Bramton, my taking you up depends entirely about what arrangement you make about Damocles. I can't pay more for the colt than I have already bid, that's "pos." I wonder if it will be possible to come to some other arrangement about it. Ha! that would do, if he would simply keep him, and let me have the management of him. He's not a man to stand on much delicacy with.

I've no doubt, to use his own vernacular, he has done a good deal of " You push my shirtings, and I'll cry up your calicoes." I must make him understand that my taking him up must be a give-and-take arrangement. The only thing is, an understanding must be come to as quickly as possible, or else, tempted by what he considers a rattling good offer, he'll be selling the colt. Hang it! Skinner was right. I shall have to play my trump card after all, and get the Countess to call. I thought I could have managed it alone, but the little dry-goods man is too cunning for me. He means that he and his are to have their legs under my mahogany, before he does what I wish. Yes, that must be my next move. I must tell the Countess to call.'

CHAPTER X.

THE SOUDAN'S ON THE BOIL.

IT is the end of the Ascot week, and a depression seems to have fallen over that lively ·community yclept the Heliotrope. They don't say much, they are mostly too good form not to take their punishment mutely, but there are wan and weary faces amongst them, that show traces of an unsuccessful week's battling with the bookmakers. The morrow is a day of rest,—little rest indeed to these unfortunates who know that their liabilities have to be adjusted on the Monday.

Sitting in one corner of the smoking-room, holding anxious confabulation on that constantly-recurring problem, ways and means, were Lord Dartree and his equally impecunious friend and mentor, Jim Anson. Suddenly their attention was attracted by a tall, dreamy-looking man, who lounged into the Temple of Nicotine with a bored, languid air, and looked wearily around for somebody on whom to inflict his weariness.

'Alec Flood! by all that's unfathomable!' exclaimed Anson. 'Come here, Alec, and tell us all about your adventures; how you escaped being bowstrung by a pasha, knouted by a Boyard, eaten by a tiger, or knifed by an Italian.'

'How are you two fellows?' replied Flood, as he shook hands with the twain. 'That last shot of yours, Jim, was a shave nearer than your guesses generally are, for I happened to be in Cairo at the time of that gambling-house row in which Dick Bramton was killed.'

'The deuce you were!' exclaimed Anson.

'Yes; your brother Jack and myself,

Dart, chanced to be present when the row took place. What took us to that confounded den, I don't know.'

'"Satan finds some mischief still for idle hands to do,"' quoted Dartree demurely.

'Stuff and nonsense, Dart!' exclaimed Jim Anson. 'Satan never bothers himself about you and Jack. He knows he can rely upon your finding that for yourselves.'

'You fellows knew Bramton, I daresay? I didn't, but Jack did, as soon as he made out who he was.'

'Rather,' said Dartree ; 'considering he owned Damocles, the first favourite for the Derby, and was always a prominent figure at Newmarket, etc., we all knew him more or less.'

'Was it a big fight ?' inquired Anson.

'No ; one of those short, sharp scuffles characteristic of a gaming-house row. This poor fellow was knifed before we could get to him. Neither of us saw who struck the blow.'

'And how's Jack?' inquired Dartree.

'Oh! flourishing. Uncommon sick of Cairo, which he pronounces a hole. Says the Sphinx and the Pyramids are all very well, once in a way, but they pall on repetition. However, he and some of the other fellows out there think they're going to fight something or somebody somewhere, and are looking forward to it. Awfully bored they must be, you know, when they are looking forward to a campaign as diversion. You fellows have been at Ascot, I suppose?'

'Yes,' replied Jim Anson; 'and, by Jove! don't we wish we hadn't. I never had such a week. Except when Damocles romped in for the New Stakes, I'm blessed if I turned a single trick; and he was only a six to four chance, so there wasn't much money to be made out of that.'

'There, that'll do, Jim; don't bore Flood by enumerating all the losers we backed at Ascot. It's sickening to look back upon. So Jack is pretty fit, is he ? When does he talk of coming home ? '

' He doesn't see his way to it at all,' rejoined Flood. ' There's trouble brewing up there in the Soudan.'

' Yes ; but that's nothing to us,' replied Lord Dartree. ' Government have declared that they are not going to interfere in the Soudan.'

' Yes, I know,' rejoined Flood. ' But when you rule an empire upon which the sun never sets, it's all very well to say you won't interfere with this, and you won't interfere with that ; you can't help yourself. Hicks' expedition to relieve El-Obeid, remember, terminated in the annihilation of his whole force. Baker's attempt to relieve Sinkat and Tokar met a precisely similar fate. Now the result of these two disasters is this—an enormous quantity of rifles and several Krupp guns and ammunition have fallen into the hands of the Arabs. Naturally a most courageous race, they have now got their tails up, and there's no holding them. They talk about sweeping the infidels from the face of the earth, and carrying fire and sword to Cairo and the gates of Stamboul. We may say that we won't interfere in the Soudan, but it's very probable that the Soudanese will interfere with us.'

' By Jove!' said Anson, 'that's a view of the case that has never struck our politicians.'

' No; we are always preaching non-intervention, and then wind up by annexing a province two or three sizes bigger than the United Kingdom. We don't want it; but circumstances compel us to take it. We don't want the Soudan, nor does any one else, I should think, but our philanthropic tendencies have led us to interfere with their favourite pastime of slave hunting, while the Egyptian officials, on the other hand, in their anxiety to enrich themselves, have ground the very souls out of the wretched villagers. No; the Soudan is on the · boil, and, to continue the metaphor, sooner or later, it will devolve upon us to take the kettle off.'

'Well, you've been out there,' said Lord Dartree, 'have heard what people say, and therefore ought to know rather more about it than we do; but nobody at home here thinks we are going to interfere in that embroglio.'

'I suppose not,' rejoined Flood; 'but when the Arabs have got within a couple of hundred miles or so of Cairo, Her Majesty's Government will awake to the situation, and exclaim, "Halloa! this sort of thing won't do, you know."'

'Well, you can't be said to take a cheerful view of things,' said Anson.

'Not at all. I'm only taking a common-sense one. Look at the blunder Government has made about the evacuation of the Soudan, loudly proclaiming their intention. When one wants to run away, one does it as quietly as possible. You don't loudly announce that you're going to do it.'

'Yes,' said Dartree, 'to retreat silently

is, I believe, an axiom in military tactics.'

'Ah! and there is another axiom in the history of both schoolboys and nations; the boy who won't fight is always kicked. Other countries are always under the impression John Bull won't fight, but too late they discover he won't be kicked. Origin this of half our wars.'

'Pity you're not in the House, Flood,' remarked Anson; 'you would make yourself so jolly unpopular, always carping at the Government arrangements.'

'Never mind,' replied the accused, laughing. 'I'm never likely to be there, and to play the critic is an easy *rôle*. However, we've talked enough of the East, I think. Tell me a little what you fellows have been doing in the West.'

'Nothing,' rejoined Lord Dartree, 'that is, speaking personally, and doing it, too, with our usual ability; haven't we, Jim?'

'Yes,' said Anson; 'but Dart has done something more than that. He has evinced great diplomatic talent. His

father, as you know, is always at him
to go in for Parliament. Well, it occurred to Dart this winter that he would
rather break his neck than his voice, and
that the society on a racecourse was more
select than the society at St Stephen's,
so he took to steeplechasing, and, I assure
you, made a very creditable *début* between
flags, carrying off two local steeplechases.'

'Yes,' chimed in Lord Dartree, 'and
the best of the joke is this, the governor
is so delighted at my taking up one of
the favourite hobbies of his youth, that
he has ceased to bore me any more
about Parliament.'

'Of course he has,' remarked Flood;
'he sees you've taken up with a higher
vocation.'

'By the way,' said Anson, 'you had no
idea, when you saw Dick Bramton killed
at Cairo, what a sensation his death was
going to make in the turf world.'

'How is that?' inquired Flood.

'Well, for a long time we couldn't
make out what was to become of his

horses. At last it oozed out he had left them all to his brother—a chap who don't know a horse from a cow. The obvious inference was that he would sell them, but he somehow discovered that race-horses are valuable property, and he is so afraid of being "done" that he can't make up his mind what to do. He made his money in trade of some sort, and he is terribly afraid of not getting full value for the stud.'

'Racing is not much in my way,' rejoined Flood, 'but one of Bramton's horses should be at all events worth money. It isn't running in his name, but that's nothing. I happened to see in the paper the other morning that Damocles won the New Stakes at Ascot. It's a very odd thing, but Dick Bramton's dying words were a message to his niece to "take care of Damocles." '

'The ruling passion,' muttered Dartree. 'My father, you know, was rather chummy with Dick Bramton, and I know from him that the dead man thought a lot of that colt. Curious, moreover, the present man has just bought a place in our part of the country.'

'Ah! I fancy I heard Jack say something about it. Now I'm off for a rubber,' and, with a nod to his companions, Flood strolled off to the cardroom.

. . . .

By this time there was a growing feeling in England that, whatever the Government might assert, their interference in the Soudan was not only imperative, but was likely to cost considerable expenditure of life and money. The disasters of Hicks and Baker had been somewhat belittled on account of the troops they were leading. These able and capable leaders, it was urged, could do nothing with the 'stuff they commanded.' We had still hardly grasped the fact that we had to confront an enemy not only of superb fighting capacity, but who, in his own way, showed great powers of strategy. Like most semi-civilised foes, his great idea was an ambuscade, and in setting and luring his opponent into his trap he showed marvellous astuteness. It was all very well to say that well-tried chiefs like Hicks and Baker, more especially the latter, whose superb handling of the Turkish rearguard in the retreat from the Balkans is worthy to rank with Ney's similar heroic covering of the Grand Armée's retirement from Moscow, could do nothing with battalions whose nervous affections of the legs impelled them to take an opposite course to that which their commanders would fain lead them. But the fierceness of the foe we were soon destined to comprehend.

The annihilation of Baker's expedition, and the literally painful cowardice displayed by the Egyptian troops upon that occasion, so emboldened Osman Digma and his Arabs that they actually now threatened Suakim ; and the British Government could no longer disguise from themselves that, if the way to India by the Suez Canal and Red Sea was to be saved, it was high time that, like it or

not, they should intervene. Sir Gerald
Graham, at the head of some six thousand British troops, was selected to chas-
tise Osman Digma and his following.
This was done, and done effectually ; but
the desperate resistance, and the reckless
charges of the Arabs, fully explained the
crushing defeats of inferior troops. How
the Arabs would fight we learnt at El-
Teb and Tamai. At the former, indeed,
a boy of twelve dauntlessly, knife in hand,
attacked two of our soldiers, paying the
penalty with his life ; while at the latter,
a square composed of some of our best
troops was momentarily broken, and the
formation not recovered till many of the
enemy had got inside, where they ' fighting fell.' But it speedily became evident
that, able as was his lieutenant, Osman
Digma the slave-dealer, with whose occu-
pation we had interfered, the focus of the
rebellion was with the Mahdi himself, and
gravitating towards Khartoum. About
the same time that Sir Gerald Graham
was chastising the tribes round Suakim,

Gordon made a sortie from the former place, the result of which was simply to show that the Egyptian troops could not be brought to face the Arabs ; two thousand of them, armed with Remingtons, being upon this occasion scattered and put to flight by some sixty wild horsemen of the desert, which made it pretty clear to Gordon, to whom had been confided the task of withdrawing the Egyptian garrisons from the Soudan, that though it might have been possible once, it was now too late, and without the aid of the British, those Egyptian troops would never return to their homes in Egypt proper. Still the Government is very determined not to intervene in the Soudan, forgetting that it has already done so, and that, having undertaken to prevent anarchy in Egypt, it was difficult to lay down hard and fast rules,— that you could no more say, 'I will be responsible for order in this part of Egypt, but not in that,' than a doctor could say, 'I will have no fever in this part of my patient's body, but will take no heed to the rest.'

However, with the suppression of Osman Digma, operations in the Soudan came to a conclusion for the present, the English Government fondly hoping that they were done with that question. True, it was urged that after the battle of Tamai there was nothing to stop Stewart's cavalry riding into Berber, but it was argued that nothing could come of such an advance; that the road from Suakim to Berber would be no safer after the cavalry had passed than it was at present, and, indeed, except the moral effect, it is hard to see what result could have come of it; but then, in dealing with Eastern nations, moral effect is everything, and if ever there were people in this world who ought to be aware of that, it is ourselves. Again and again have we owed our existence in India to our military prestige; and had the matter been left in the hands of the military chiefs, it is probable that Berber would have been occupied; and who shall say what moral support would have been afforded Gordon at Khartoum by the intelligence that the British horse were in Berber? But no, the British Government were excessively anxious to wash their hands of this question of the Soudan, but found that, once having tarred its fingers, it was a matter of no little difficulty to get rid of it. As it is, the affair does not redound much to our credit, as the problem has been elucidated by the massacre of all the Egyptian garrisons, and the shameful sacrifice of the man we sent out to withdraw them.

CHAPTER XI.

THE BRAMTONS MAKE THEIR DÉBUT.

Not very far from Temple Rising was Roseneath, the residence of Mr and Mrs Berriman. Mr Berriman was a man who somewhat startled the inhabitants of that neighbourhood by his ultra-democratic opinions. It was a strongly Conservative district, and when he first came amongst them there had been some feeling against the master of Roseneath on account of his very Liberal views; but when it was discovered that he was a thorough good sportsman, a staunch preserver of both pheasants and foxes, and that his Radical opinions were chiefly theoretical, he speedily became a popular man in the county. As for Mrs Berriman, she was a jolly, good-tempered woman, who delighted in society, and was very catholic regarding it. There was nothing exclusive about Mrs Berriman; she knew everybody, and dispensed her hospitalities with a free hand. Her manner was just as frank and off-hand to the Earl of Ranksborow as it was to the village apothecary. That Mrs Berriman should call upon the newcomers at Temple Rising, was as natural as that Mrs Berriman should give a garden-party. Mrs Berriman's parties were always popular. True some of the more exclusive people of the neighbourhood—the very finest porcelain of the community—turned up their noses at the inferior earthenware they encountered on such occasions, but having remarked that 'poor Mrs Berriman's parties were really getting so very mixed, they didn't know what to say about going,' they went.

The Bramtons looked forward to this entertainment not a little. It was a

stepping-stone to making the acquaintance
of the neighbourhood. John Bramton and
his wife were naturally both sociable and
hospitable people, and would be only
too happy to dispense cakes and ale to
their neighbours, if only those neighbours
would let them.

Now a thing had come to pass, the
last two or three weeks, at which Mr
Bramton hardly knew whether to be
pleased or annoyed. When this much-
talked-of colt Damocles cantered in for the
New Stakes at Ascot, there was of course
much talk about whom he belonged to.
He had run in the name of the trainer,
but it was pretty generally understood that
Stubber was not his real owner, and it
then transpired that the horse was the
property of Mr Bramton. This, as we
know, was not exactly the case, but it
seemed so natural that the dead man
should have left his property to his
brother, that nobody dreamt of question-
ing the statement. Mr Stubber himself
was quite under that impression, and saw

no object in making a secret of it ; equally
are Mr Skinner and the Earl of Ranksborow under that belief, so it is very
little wonder that Mr Bramton is regarded
as the owner of Damocles.

'Pwoperty of a wetired linen-dwaper,
I'm told,' ejaculated young Pontifex of
the —th Dragoon Guards, as he joined
the drag to which he was affiliated for
luncheon.

He had not backed the winner, and
his own father had been a cheesemonger,
whereas Mr Bramton had, at all events,
been a wholesale dealer in such goods
as he traded in.

Two or three of the sporting farmers,
and some of the few of the gentlemen
around, when they met Mr Bramton, had
congratulated him upon the triumph of his
horse at Ascot, some of them adding in a
jocular way that they supposed next year
the bells would be ringing at Temple
Rising, an ox would be roasted whole,
and a hogshead of home-brewed broached,
in honour of the victory of Damocles at

Epsom. Now Mr Bramton took all this very awkwardly. Guided by the lights of his whole life, he felt that to be the possessor of a racehorse boded his destruction; that men would stand aloof from him; and, though he didn't quite understand how, yet that there was a great expenditure of money connected with the ownership of this sort of property. That was his theory, but his shrewd common-sense showed him the reverse was the case. He could not but see that his sporting neighbours looked upon it as quite a feather in his cap to be the owner of such a 'flyer' as Damocles. Mr Stubber, in a letter which he had received from him, congratulated him upon having won fifteen hundred pounds in stakes, on his horse having distinctly established himself as a first-class two-year-old, and again asseverating that the value he had placed upon him a fortnight ago was not a penny too much, and imploring him not to be tempted to sell.

'If, sir,' continued Mr Stubber, 'you will allow me to advise, I would suggest, if you do not want to continue racing, your putting up the stud for sale during the July Week, with the exception of Damocles and old Whitechapel, whom I want to lead him in his work.' ('Now I wonder what he means by that?' muttered Mr Bramton to himself, as he perused the letter.) 'The young one is as sound as a bell, and, I assure you, bids fair to be a perfect gold mine to you.'

Now Mr Bramton could quite understand all this. It was very pleasant to learn that his property was improving in value—or rather his daughter's—to learn that they had won a stake worth fifteen hundred pounds; and then he thought it was very odd that it hadn't been sent to him, and remarked to himself that if that was the way Royalty did business, he could only remark that it was somewhat lax; then he wondered whether the Queen or the Chancellor of the Exchequer was the proper person to write to on the subject, and finally concluded that he had better take council with the Earl of Ranksborow.

Between this nobleman and Mr Bramton there had been much finessing. The Countess had called, and, loyal to her husband's instructions, had skilfully dangled the bait of a dinner at Knightshayes before the eyes of the family; but she had not named the day. On the other hand, Mr Bramton had been equally indefinite on the subject of Damocles. He did not altogether decline the Earl's offer, but then he most distinctly did not accept it. The nobleman did not like to stir much in the matter. He had got to the length of his tether, and knew he was offering nothing like the value of the horse. He was afraid that Bramton already suspected as much, and to press the offer would only confirm those suspicions. But time went on. As Artemus Ward remarks, 'It's a way time has.' Damocles won the New Stakes, and then Lord Ranksborow recognised that to purchase him was out of his power. His sole hope now was to get the control of the horse. That, he thought, should not be very difficult. Mr Bramton, knowing nothing about racing, would probably feel flattered and grateful to a man like himself for taking the management of his 'crack' off his hands. Then, again, he knew the Temple Rising people set a high value on the friendship of Knightshayes, so that the Earl announced to his Countess *that dinner* must become a reality, and that as soon as, with regard to due notice being given, could be managed. Having failed to buy the colt himself, the next thing was to persuade John Bramton on no account to part with it.

'We must do it, Louisa. I have too much depending on Damocles winning next year, to throw away any chance conducive to it. It won't bore you very much. As for the Miss Bramtons, they are pleasant, ladylike girls enough, and though the father and the mother are atrociously vulgar, yet they're so *naïve* with it, that it becomes more amusing than offensive.'

'Oh! I sha'n't mind it,' laughed her ladyship. 'The only one trouble about it is their charming *naïveté* is somewhat provocative of laughter, and the Miss Bramtons, bear in mind, are jealously sensitive about their parents' mistakes.'

'You may quite rely upon me upon that point,' rejoined the Earl, 'though they try one rather high at times.'

'That's settled, then,' rejoined the Countess. 'I'll write at once, and ask them to dine here Friday week. I shall meet them, most likely, at the Berrimans'. All the neighbourhood will be there to-morrow, I suppose?'

'Except myself,' replied the Earl. 'However, Berriman does the thing well, and all that can be made of a garden-party will be done.'

The Temple Rising people were very pleased with their *début* at Roseneath. Good-natured Mrs Berriman never did things by halves, and she introduced the

Bramtons in all directions. Mankind is prone to novelty, and the girls being pretty and attractive, soon drew several admirers to their side ; amongst these was Sir Kenneth Sandiman.

Sir Kenneth was a man about forty, who having pretty well dissipated the small inheritance with which he began life, was now seeking to repair his fortunes by a wealthy marriage. He had already heard of the Bramtons, and no sooner did he set his eyes on the girls than he thought his opportunity was come. He was a proud, conceited man, with an exaggerated idea of his own importance. He had never distinguished himself in any way, and really carried very little weight in his own county or anywhere else. The baronetcy was an old one, and had he felt free to wed according to the dictates of his nature, Sir Kenneth would have aspired to alliance with the peerage. As it was, he must marry money, and he considered that the transforming of Miss Bramton

into Lady Sandiman was an honour quite
sufficient to turn the head of either girl.
A tradesman, as he argued superciliously,
who could afford to buy Temple Rising
must be rich. The girls really were very
pretty, and inquiry told him there was
no son. Yes, it would do very well; old
Bramton would doubtless be delighted to
give his daughters handsome *dots* if they
married to his satisfaction, and it wasn't
likely they could hope to be anything
higher than Lady Sandiman. The idea
of a rebuff never even entered Sir Kenneth's head. There was only one difficulty, which he confidentially told Mrs
Berriman.

'I can't see any myself,' returned his
hostess bluntly, with all a good-natured
woman's wish to forward a suitable marriage. 'You're just the age, Sir Kenneth,
that a man ought to settle down. Either
of those girls would bring you a good
lump of money, and do you credit as
a wife.'

'My dear Mrs Berriman, you don't

quite understand me,' said the fastidious baronet; 'the trouble is, I can't make up my mind which I admire most.'

'Upon my word,' rejoined his hostess, 'I don't think that need trouble you this afternoon. You can't possibly expect to make such rapid progress as to render any decision on that point necessary to-day.'

'I don't know,' rejoined Sir Kenneth languidly. 'Eligible men with a position to offer are soon snapped up in these times.'

'Pooh! Sir Kenneth,' replied Mrs Berriman, 'don't you talk about position, and all that sort of thing, to democrats like us. Don't you know that my husband is an advanced Radical, who is all for doing away with titles and such like frivolities.'

'Just so,' replied the imperturbable baronet. 'Government will make him a baronet some day, and then you'll see how he'll change his opinions.'

Mrs Berriman shook her fan merrily at him as she replied,—

'You'd better go and have a good think, and, when you've made up your mind, commence your courtship. I have introduced you, so that everything lies at your own discretion.'

'Well, Mrs B.,' said John Bramton, in an undertone, 'how are you getting on with the aristocracy? A more affable set of gents I never saw in my life; but they seem to think a deal more of me as the owner of Damocles than as the owner of Temple Rising. I'll tell you what, my dear, it's getting awkward. On the strength of that blessed horse, they will have it that I'm a sportsman; one of the right sort they say. Well, I hope so; but I don't feel very sure about keeping it up. What do you think, I have promised to subscribe to the hounds.'

'Oh! John, what made you do that? You know you were never out hunting in your life.'

'No; but I haven't said anything about following them, you know. This keeping up the character of a real sportsman is rather expensive, Margaret. There was another fellow said he knew I'd give them a pony for their local races, and when I said that I didn't happen to have such a thing in the stable at present, he poked me in the ribs, and said, " I would have my little joke, and that he should put me down for twenty-five pounds," and, what is more, he did ! '

'Well,' said Mrs Bramton, 'I suppose one must subscribe to all these sort of things when one lives in the country.'

'The country seems to think so. There's a parson who got hold of me, hoped I would allow him to put me down for the cricket club; had no doubt I played. However, I lost no time in dispelling that illusion. I told him he could put me down for the club, but added emphatically that I only looked on. There was another fellow, too, very anxious to discuss a division of the water with me, and when I told him that he might have it all as I didn't do much in that way, he thanked me profusely, and said it was the best stretch of fishing in the county. I'm rather sorry I gave it him now, for if I am to set up as a sportsman, fishing strikes me as the safest line to come out in !' and then Mr Bramton strolled away again, to be once more bewildered by the attentions of his sporting neighbours, who could not be convinced that the brother of so well-known a racing man as Richard Bramton could be anything but a gentleman learned in horse-flesh, and of sporting tendencies.

Sir Kenneth Sandiman, meanwhile, had commenced operations in good earnest. He had walked Miss Bramton clear of the general crowd, and, having disposed of the usual conventionalities customary in our first intercourse with strangers, was fast settling down into an incipient flirtation with his fair companion. Matilda Bramton was no novice at the game— quite able to take care of herself, and as much disposed to while away an hour or two in this harmless amusement as her cavalier. She laughed at his pretty speeches, and put but little value upon them; and when they parted, mutually well pleased with each other, nobody would have felt more astonished than herself if she had been told that Sir Kenneth Sandiman had serious intentions concerning her.

CHAPTER XII.

THE DINNER AT KNIGHTSHAYES.

'WELL, Lucy, what did you think of our party to-day?' inquired Miss Bramton, as she came into her sister's room, just previous to dressing for dinner.

'They were a pleasant lot of people, and seem inclined to be civil. There was one thing rather interested me, and that was I heard Lady Ranksborow telling Mrs Berriman that Mr Flood had returned to England. He is evidently well known down here.'

'Flood—Mr Flood? Ah! I remember. One of the gentlemen who took care of you in Cairo. More to the purpose, my sister, if it had been the other who had come home, wouldn't it ? '

'I don't suppose it much matters, but I saw a good deal more of Captain Cuxwold than I did of Mr Flood. However, they were both as kind as they knew how to be.'

'Well, I've no experience of soldiers ; but they've a general reputation for being rather good at making themselves agreeable when they choose. What did you think of my cavalier, Sir Kenneth ? '

'He was extremely attentive ; in fact, quite as devoted as it was possible for a man to be at a first interview. I should say, Matilda, he was rather struck with you ! '

'Oh, you goose !' said Miss Bramton, laughing merrily ; 'that's only his natural manner. Sir Kenneth can't help it. He is one of those men who would make love to a petticoat if he met it on a clothes-line. He is a confirmed flirt, and, I should think, never had serious intentions in his life. However, he was very pleasant this afternoon. Was there any talk of Mr Flood's coming down here?'

'Not that I heard,' replied Lucy; 'in fact, all I discovered about him was what I told you.'

Now it was an odd thing, but it had never as yet occurred to Lucy to connect the Captain Cuxwold she had met in Cairo with the Ranksborow family; firstly, she had no idea that he was entitled to the preface of the Honourable Captain Cuxwold; and secondly, until this afternoon, she had really not known the Earl of Ranksborow's family name. The presence of Lady Jane and Lady Emily Cuxwold at Mrs Berriman's party had certainly opened her eyes, and made her speculate as to whether the dragoon she had known at Cairo was any connection of the Ranksborow family, but it still never occurred to her that he was a junior scion of the house. Neither she nor her sister were much given to a study of the peerage; although the probability was that they would now, at all events, read

up the Ranksborow tree, if only to ascertain the exact ages of Lady Jane and Lady
Emily,—there being always much exulta-
tion in the feminine mind on convicting a
sister of a year or two more than she ac-
knowledges.   Lucy most certainly would
have liked to meet Mr Flood, if only for
the purpose of inquiring about his friend ;
but she had heard nothing that led her to
believe that his appearance in Barkshire
was expected at present.

As for Mr Bramton, the result of the
Berrimans' party had been most titillating
to his vanity.   He had found himself
looked upon as a man of no little importance, but he was too shrewd not to see
that the possession of Damocles weighed
heavily in the estimation of his neighbours.   There was no question now of
selling the horses ; on the contrary, he
felt so proud of the distinction that the
owning of a racing stud seemed to confer
upon him, that he quite forgot it was the
property of his daughter and not of himself.   The neighbourhood was determined

to regard him as a sportsman. He was not the first man whom circumstances have thrust into a *rôle* for which they are perfectly unfitted; but it was no use denying it. Disclaims on his part were only met with polite incredulity, and, with the exception perhaps of the Earl of Ranksborow, there were none who did not believe that John Bramton was a good all-round sportsman, but especially that he was a very knowing hand about turf matters. Several men that afternoon had sought to draw him into racing conversation; his reticence thereon, which was due merely to ignorance, was put down to astuteness, and they one and all believed that he could tell them a good deal if he chose to speak.

Ah! how often we are condemned out of our own mouths; how many of us might be credited with wisdom if we could but hold our tongues.

One thing certainly filled Mr Bramton with misgivings, how was he to keep up this cheaply-won reputation? He knew he could not sustain it in the saddle, and he was conscious of having accepted sundry hazily-defined invitations to 'shoot when the season began.' True there were rather over two months before, as he remarked to himself, that casualty could occur, but he could not disguise, as he thought of these invitations, that his knowledge of firearms went no further than shooting for nuts at a fair. The last words of the gentleman whom he had unintentionally obliged about the fishing had been, 'Of course I'll drop you a re-minder; but mind you're pledged to come to me on the first.'

'Can't say where I may be on the first,' murmured Mr Bramton, 'but it certainly won't be at the house of that bloodthirsty bird-slayer.'

But there was another section of the turf world vastly moved and puzzled by Mr John Bramton's movements. Mr Skinner had been duly informed by his employer of his utter failure to purchase Damocles, and he in his turn informed the

Earl that there was a growing anxiety to know what Mr Bramton meant to do with those horses.

'Resolves itself,' said Mr Skinner, 'into the great fact that your lordship has got all the yearling books about the colt, and, judging by his *début*, it looks very much as if he had a great chance of winning the Derby. Now you will excuse my saying that your lordship didn't exercise your usual discretion when you accepted twenty thousand to three hundred from James Noel. It is very rarely that anybody wins long odds from him, and, though as long as the colt is with Stubber no harm will come to him that his trainer can possibly guard against, yet there's something in what one of the most straightforward bookmakers said in my hearing only yesterday about Damocles, "We needn't bother our heads much about that one. Jim Noel has laid him, and it's wonderful how a horse comes to grief when Jim has laid long odds against him."'

The Earl was much exercised about this letter. He had never stood to win such a stake over a horse in his life as he did over Damocles for next year's Derby. He knew Mr James Noel—nobody better—and could but admit that there was reason in what Skinner told him. As for Bramton, he hadn't quite made up his mind about him. That the man was sharp enough he had no doubt, that he knew anything about racing he thought extremely questionable; if he did, then all he could say was that John Bramton played the innocent better than any man he had ever seen. But his own opinion was that his ignorance was not feigned; and yet, the Earl reflected, the owner of Temple Rising seemed to have determined to act on his own judgment in racing matters. However, the Earl's stay at Knightshayes was drawing to a close; but before it was over, it had been arranged that the Bramtons should dine there. The Ranksborows were people who broke the London season by taking an occasional run down to their country seat. On the present occasion the Countess and her daughters had come down for a somewhat prolonged edition of the Whitsuntide holidays, and the Earl had joined them at Knightshayes after the termination of the Ascot week. At this dinner Lord Ranksborow felt that, if possible, he must come to some arrangement with his guest about the control of Damocles. The colt was entered in the July Stakes at Newmarket as well as having two or three engagements at Goodwood; and from the style in which he had won on the Royal Heath, it did not seem likely that the penalty he was rendered liable to by his Ascot victory would interfere with his success for whatever he might be elected to run. Now this was exactly the control that the Earl wished to possess—the deciding for what races Damocles should compete—and although buying the colt was out of his power, he thought it very possible that he might fill the place of turf-adviser to John Bramton. In good sooth no one was better calculated for the post. He was not only an astute and veteran turfite, but, in the present instance, his interests and John Bramton's lay in the same direction. The Earl had been much too long at the game not to re-cognise the truth of the old axiom that 'A bet is never a bet till it is hedged.' Standing as he did to win an enormous stake over Damocles, the more that colt distinguished himself in his two-year - old career, the better it would serve his turn ; every race the horse won would shorten the price against him for next year's Derby, and afford the Earl the opportunity of attaining that halcyon, though rarely experienced, state of things known as ' standing on velvet,' whereby is, of course, meant the standing to win a comfortable stake with no pos-sibility of loss. As before said, the Earl regarded Mr Bramton as unfeignedly ig-norant of racing. He looked on Stubber the trainer as a straightforward, honest man, who could be thoroughly trusted to do his duty with the horses under his charge; but when it came to pitting Stubber against such a perfectly un-scrupulous turf tactician as Mr James Noel, Lord Ranksborow regarded it as pretty much the country yokel playing against a thimblerigger.

'Stubber,' he muttered, 'is no doubt straight enough; but Noel, if he couldn't get at the horse in the stable, would get at the jockey out. No; a man wants to be master of every move on the board to play against him. If I can, I'll play my own hand!'

The dinner party duly came off, and no sooner had the ladies left the room than Lord Ranksborow exclaimed,—

'Come up to my end of the table, Bramton. I want to have a racing palaver with you. Why, I've hardly had an opportunity of congratulating you about Damocles' victory in the New Stakes.'

'Very good of your lordship, I'm sure. I'm sorry I couldn't oblige your lordship; but the fact is—'

'I'd no idea how good he was,' interrupted the Earl, in an easy, off-hand manner; 'and didn't offer you above a quarter his value. Your brother was a rattling good judge, and I knew he had a very high opinion of the colt. I know two things more now; first, that your brother was quite right, and, secondly, that I can't afford to buy Damocles.'

'No judge of these things myself, but I suppose that horse is worth a tidy sum. Now, what should you say, my lord?'

'Couldn't price him at all, Bramton. He's worth a lot more than I offered you for him; but I hope your not thinking of selling him. Let's bring the Blue Ribbon to Barkshire, though I can't afford to pay for the luxury of winning it.'

'Well,' said John Bramton, as he sipped his port, 'I've always found in business it's a mistake, you know, to stand out too long. It's always difficult to know when the top of the market is reached. You make a good spec' say, and buy goods at 80; they run up to 115, and you say at 120 I'll sell; then comes a sudden drop, and you are perhaps glad to take 90 or so after all.'

' I hope you'll allow me to guide you a little in this matter. You mustn't think of selling the colt yet. I assure you there's a lot of money to be made out of him. Now, for instance, there are the July Stakes next month. I suppose you'll run him for that ? '

' I'm sure I don't know. I didn't know that he was in for such a thing. I've never even seen him yet. By the way, I don't want to make any scandal, but, you know, I haven't heard anything about that money I won at Ascot yet. I suppose I had better write about it ? '

' I've not the slightest doubt Messrs Weatherby in Old Burlington Street have placed it to your account,' replied the Earl, laughing. 'You must come down to New-market next month and see your colt run.'

'Ah! I suppose it is the proper thing to do when you're an owner of racehorses,' and Mr Bramton thrust his thumbs into the armholes of his waistcoat and threw himself into his favourite pompous attitude; 'but I leave most of the arrangements to Stubber, my fellow, you know—sort of medical man in charge of the horses, keeps 'em in health, and all that sort of thing.'

'I know him. Excellent man. No better trainer at Newmarket; but it is as well to look after these sort of things yourself.'

'Quite so, quite so,' replied Mr Bramton. 'The only thing is when you're no judge of the goods, by which I mean the horses, it's best to leave the buying and selling, by which I mean the settling what they're to do, to somebody who understands the business. Now, my lord, the only thing I can understand is putting these horses up to auction, and letting 'em go for what they will fetch. Stubber recommends me to do that, and I've told him to arrange to do it next month.'

'God bless my soul! man,' exclaimed the Earl excitedly, 'you don't mean to say you are going to put Damocles up for sale next month?'

'Bramton is joking,' cried Mr Berriman, who had been listening to the conversation with no little curiosity. 'You can't mean to deprive Barkshire of the honour of taking its first Derby?'

'You didn't let me finish,' said John Bramton. 'Stubber advised me to sell the whole stud, bar Damocles and a horse called Whitechapel, which, it seems, he thinks necessary to "lead the work," whatever that may mean.'

Mr Berriman and the Earl laughed, and the former said:

'It won't do, Bramton; it won't do. Fellows talk "horse" very often who know precious little about it, but you don't catch me taking long odds from a fellow who pretends to know as little about it as you do. Bless you, my boy,

I've been had by the innocents in my day.
We know all about the Heathen Chinee
and the game "he did not understand."'

If Berriman and the Earl did, Bramton
did not. He had been a busy man all
his life till quite lately, and his reading
had been pretty strictly confined to the
daily papers, and, as we know, there were
some parts of those at which he never
glanced. But one thing Bramton did
understand, and that was that the general
public were determined to regard him as
a sportsman, and that his affectation of
ignorance on the subject was regarded as
a capital joke. In racing matters this is so
constantly the case, that the man who knows
nothing, and maintains a rigid silence, is
always regarded as a model of astuteness,
and when, considerably more to his own
surprise than that of anybody else, the
horse which he has not backed for a six-
pence wins easily, he is credited with having won an enormous stake, and having
been a very Mephistophiles in the manipulation of the betting market.

CHAPTER XIII.

LUCY'S INNOCULATION.

LORD RANKSBOROW, as they joined the ladies, was hardly satisfied with the results of his diplomatic dinner. Mr Bramton, while quite admitting that his ignorance of racing distinctly unfitted him to determine for what stakes Damocles should run, yet by no means seemed desirous of handing over such decision to his host. Mr Bramton, in his business days, had been apt to reckon up his fellows pretty accurately. He had come to the conclusion that Mr Stubber was an honest, energetic man, who knew what he was about, and he thought it just as well that the management of the colt should be left entirely to him. The Earl had sounded his guest pretty freely on this point; but though John Bramton temporised, and did not positively decline to accept Lord Ranksborow's proffered services, yet he never for one second committed himself, and boldly made the request which the Earl had hoped, namely, that he would take the entire management of Damocles. He would go no further than saying that he was extremely fortunate to have a friend like his lordship, to whom he could always come for advice, but he would not pledge himself even not to sell the colt. He would go no further than say he should not part with him at present. He would hear what Stubber had to say after the others were sold, etc. In fact, the Earl rather ruefully came to the conclusion that John Bramton meant to take his own way in this business, and that his trainer would probably have more to say to the tactics of the stable than any one else.

'A deuced knowing shot this,' mused

the Earl, 'and perfectly able to take care of himself. They'll not get Temple Rising out of him as they did from poor Moly- neux; but, shrewd as he is, he has one weak point, and that point might cost him a lot of money, as it has done many others. He has a tremendous idea of his own importance, and that will be my safeguard about his sticking to Damocles. He has already discovered that owning the first favourite of the Derby adds to his importance. It will be easy to keep that feeling alive in a dozen different ways, and as long as his pocket is not touched too severely, he'll not forego the swagger of the position.'

In the course of the evening the Miss Bramtons were also made conscious of the pleasures of owning successful race- horses. Several trophies in the way of cups decorated both the dinner-table and the sideboard, which had been won by the Earl in the course of his turf career. Lady Jane Cuxwold, too, showed a hand- some bracelet which her father had given her upon the occasion of his winning the Chester Cup some four years ago. The Earl was lavish to his family when fortune smiled upon him ; and when they saw the interest the Miss Bramtons took in it, the Countess as well as her daughters exhibited various specimens of the spoils of war.

Lady Ranksborow was not a little struck by the keen, sensible inquiries that Lucy Bramton made about turf matters. The girl evidently knew but little about them, but she was very persistent in her endeavours to understand the mysteries of racing. Her sister, on the other hand, gabbled on as young ladies are somewhat wont to do, saying it must be delightful to win races and get bangles, and that she was quite sure that she should delight in it; that she had never seen anything of it yet ; but that, now her uncle had left them his stud, of course they should go everywhere.

Now it must be borne in mind that though Mrs and Miss Bramton were per-

fectly well aware that Richard Bramton's
property had been all left to Lucy, yet
they never proclaimed that fact, and were
indeed honestly ignorant that these racehorses were not only hers, but that it was
an open question whether they were not
under her own immediate control; that
she could positively decide for what stakes
they should run; and that it would be a
fine point for the lawyers whether Lucy,
for instance, had not the right to strike
Damocles out of all engagements. The
young lady was very quiet, but she had
a will of her own. Her uncle's money
she knew must come positively into her
own possession when she came of age,
and, besides the desire to carry out her
uncle's last wishes, her imagination had
been highly inflamed by the victory of
Damocles at Ascot. Then these Ranksborow people, who had all been brought
up amidst the racecourse and the hunting field, still further excited her, and
she began to think that it would be
rather a fine thing to be the owner of

a few racehorses. Under the tuition of
Lady Jane and Lady Emily, she made
considerable progress in turf lore. That
evening she ascertained that there was
nothing out of the way in a lady keeping some, though they usually ran them
in an assumed name; and the result of
all this talk was that Lucy resolved to
ascertain at once how far her control really
extended over Mr Stubber's charges. For
instance, she knew her father was contemplating the sale of the greater part
of them. At all events she would write
to Mr Pecker, and have a legal opinion
as to whether this could be done in op-
position to her wishes, should she think
fit to decree otherwise. However, in the
meantime, the appearance of the gentlemen changed the tenor of the conversation, and Miss Bramton, at all events,
was soon immersed in her flirtation with
Sir Kenneth Sandiman.

'Nice affable people the Ranksborows,'
said Mr Bramton, as they drove home.
'Not a bit stuck up. Being an owner of

racehorses, you see, gives one a sort of tone in society, I find. Bless you! they all seem to regard me as an authority.'

'I don't see much use in it, if we're never to go and see races,' rejoined Miss Bramton, rather sharply. 'Lady Jane told me they always went to Ascot, and was quite surprised that we were not there to see Damocles win.'

'Yes, papa, and they would not believe that we had never even seen him. I must see Damocles,' said Lucy, with quiet but decided emphasis ; and the girl was more than ever confirmed in her resolve to write to Mr Pecker on the morrow.

'Yes, John ; we really must go to the next fashionable gathering. I don't know when it is, or where it is, but we must go.'

'Yes ; and it's the proper thing to give your daughters bracelets or something of that sort when you win, papa!' exclaimed Matilda.

'Yes ; and you must win, and you must do it,' chorused Lucy.

'I tell you what it is,' said Mr Bramton testily, 'if an owner of racehorses is liable to all these obligations, the sooner I'm out of the lot the better.'

'Oh! you can't do that, papa. Lady Ranksborow said she was sure you were too good a sportsman to part with Damocles before he had won the Derby.'

'Well,' said Mr Bramton, 'I'm not sure I'm quite calculated to make a good sportsman ; it seems that there is a little too much expected of one. Now, as far as a quiet day's fishing goes, I don't mind ; but this subscribing to the hounds, etc., I don't exactly see.'

'All quite necessary in your position, papa dear,' said Miss Matilda. 'I'm sure we've had a most delightful evening, and Sir Kenneth is a most agreeable man, worth a hundred of those old business frumps or young City prigs you used to bring home to dinner at Wimbledon.'

John Bramton relapsed into silence. The contest was too unequal—the ladies were all against him—and he found himself, so to speak, under such a cross-fire of conversation that the holding of his tongue was the most discreet thing he could do ; and in spite of the elation the being the reputed owner of Damocles had occasioned him during the evening, he thought, perhaps, that the sooner he got rid of the horses, which he had now quite learned to consider his own, the better.

'What does Dartree say ?' inquired the Earl, as he entered his wife's room, and found the Countess glancing over a letter in her son's handwriting.

'I was so late that I hadn't time to read it before dinner,' replied Lady Ranksborow ; 'but there's nothing much in it, unless you consider this message to you of importance. " Tell my father," he says, "that Damocles is very unsteady in the market. There's a tendency to lay against him in somewhat dangerous quarters. No reason that I can hear of except they say that he will be offered for sale during the July week. Ask him if he knows anything about it." '

'Know anything about it,' said the Earl irritably. 'I know as much about it as it's possible to know with such a suspicious, undecided fool as Bramton to deal with.'

'I think you're wrong there, Rank,' said the Countess. 'It strikes me Mr Bramton is no fool, whatever else he may be.'

'No, you're quite right, he isn't ; but he's so afraid of anybody getting the better of him, of his not making the very most of these horses, that it's impossible to wring a decided answer out of him about what he's going to do with Damocles. He has eaten my mutton and drank my claret,' continued the Earl, laughing, 'under false pretences to-night. I asked him here for the purpose of getting a distinct declaration of his views on that very point. I wanted him to let me have the management of the horse ; but no, all I could get out of him was that he had not as yet made up his mind to sell Damocles, which I knew before.'

'You and Dart stand to win a big stake over this horse, don't you ?'

'Yes.'

'And would rather he remained in Mr Bramton's hands than otherwise?'

'Just so,' said the Earl, with a nod.

'Then you leave it to me and the girls, Rank. You needn't laugh; we can do more for you than you think here. Jane and Emily, without intending it, have given the Miss Bramtons the racing fever to-night. We'll take care it don't cool. They'll never let their father sell Damocles.'

Lord Ranksborow laughed.

'All right,' he rejoined; 'do your best. Remember, if Damocles won, next day there would be an easiness in the money market to which for years we've been unaccustomed.'

True to her resolve, the next morning Lucy wrote to Mr Pecker to inquire how her powers stood with regard to this proposed sale. Mr Pecker's answer, which arrived in the course of two or three days, was clear and succinct.

'With regard to the greater part of

these horses, no question arises. The condition of the will is, till they have run through their engagements. Most of them have been nominated by the late Richard Bramton, and such nominations are void by his death. Damocles and another two-year-old called Lucifer, both heavily engaged, are nominated by Mr Stubber, as also, it appears, is a five-year-old named Whitechapel, in one or two instances. The question, therefore, of your power to keep or sell under the codicil are confined to these three ; and, in the case of the latter horse, it will speedily expire, as his engagements will be fulfilled. With Damocles and Lucifer the case is very different, as their engagements extend over the whole of next year, and even into the year beyond, I have taken counsel's opinion, and the result is that, though admittedly a very fine point, the authority I consulted thinks the codicil goes beyond a wish, and implies a condition of inheritance which might be legally disputed if not complied with. As far as we know, there is nobody to raise the question; but, as a lawyer, I must say, "*Don't give a possible somebody the chance.*" My racing experiences are of little value, but my advice to you would be to let these horses run through engagements at the discretion of their trainer. Mr Stubber has the credit of being a clever, straightforward man in his business, and, from what he told me, Damocles will more than pay all expenses.'

Bitten as Lucy was, but in much more genuine fashion than her father, with a strong inclination to dabble with the turf, this letter was eminently satisfactory. With her father, the possession or control of racehorses was merely a thing he desired because it increased his importance; but Lucy's imagination had been excited by the Ladies Cuxwold, and she had begun to dream of seeing her own horse and her own colours at Ascot, Goodwood, or some of the great turf social gatherings. Mr Pecker's letter

told her that it behoved her to keep
three of the horses, and amongst them
Damocles, which, from what her uncle
had told her, and from what she had
heard since, she believed to be much
the best horse she possessed ; and, indeed, it was to him she looked for the
attainment of such social successes as
she might attain on the racecourse. She
looked forward to the time when she
might become the heroine of the hour ;
when she might be pointed out as the
owner of Damocles, who had just won
the principal race at Sandown. She had
read only a little before that the Mar-
chioness of Budleigh had appeared in the
royal paddock at Ascot attired in a dress
of her husband's racing colours. Then
she wondered what Uncle Dick's colours
were ; and then came woman's natural
hope that they were pretty—thinking over
as she was this matter of a dress of the
same colours, it was highly essential that
they should be so. For instance, she had
read in this very account of somebody's

well-known jacket of white and green spots proving triumphant. Now, what was any woman to make of a dress of that description ? However, she supposed colours could be changed like other things ; and then, I'm afraid, it occurred to her feminine and uninstructed mind that it might be nice to change her colours as she did her dresses, or, at all events, once every season. She had yet to learn that a thorough turfite is devoted to his jacket —as proud of the banner which he had seen borne triumphant in a hundred frays as the soldier of the colours under which he has fought and bled.

Then she fell to ruminating on Mr Pecker's letter. Armed with that, she felt she could defy her father, who, though flattered, as above said, by the importance the ownership of Damocles conferred upon him, was too keen a money-maker not to sell the horse for a large sum if the matter rested entirely with him. As a matter of sport, Mr Bramton felt no manner of interest in the inheritance that had come to his daughter; as a matter of swagger, he no doubt did. But Lucy knew that her father's old business habits would eclipse that as soon as the bait dangled before his eyes was big enough. Armed with Mr Pecker's letter, she felt that she could do as she liked with her own, although a good year must elapse before she attained her majority.

CHAPTER XIV.

MR SKINNER IS PUZZLED.

'WELL, Stubber,' exclaimed Mr Skinner, as he encountered the trainer coming home with his string from the Heath on the Monday in the July week, 'I see Dick Bramton's horses are all up for sale, bar Damocles ?'

'Not quite,' replied the other as he walked his cob alongside the commissioner's hack. 'My new employer has kept Damocles, and Whitechapel to lead him, at my request; but I'll tell you one thing more, Mr John Bramton may know nothing about things, but there is somebody pulling the strings who does. I wonder who has recommended him to keep Lucifer—never suggested it—but whoever did is a good judge.'

'Promising, eh?' remarked Skinner.

'Yes; he is a smartish colt, though backward. I've never been able to try him properly yet, but I've no doubt, before the end of the season, he will show himself what I tell you.'

'I suppose Mr Bramton never comes down to look at the horses?'

'Never been down since they were his,' rejoined the trainer; 'never had an employer in my life who took so little interest in racing. I went to see him once, and I've written to him several times, and telegraphed to him besides, but I've only had one letter from him, and that was to tell me that I was to put all the horses up for sale this week, with the exception of the three mentioned. I'm very glad he's going to stick to Damocles, and I'm glad he keeps Lucifer; but what prompted him to keep the latter, I'm jiggered if I know.'

'It is odd where he got that hint,'

remarked Skinner. 'Why, even I, who am always at it, didn't know that you reckoned Lucifer smart. Of course I knew you had got a colt of that name. Lucifer by Satan, out of Morning Star, is pretty heavily entered, but the very horse-watchers haven't begun to talk about him yet.'

'No; and he won't be seen out till the back end. If Mr Bramton had been a racing gentleman, I should have told him not to part with that one, but I was so afraid of his putting Damocles up for sale, that I didn't like to go too far. Dam'me, he looks upon racehorses as not only expensive, but dangerous besides.'

'Well, good-bye, Stubber. I must go home and get some breakfast. I don't suppose the penalty will stop your colt in the Julys.'

'Not a bit of it,' laughed the trainer; 'he could carry five pound more, and win. Take advice, and though it is contrary to your rule, stand the favourite for once.'

'I think I must,' replied the bookmaker,

smiling, 'if the odds on him are not too expensive. Good-morning. I'd give a sovereign,' muttered Mr Skinner to himself, 'to know what induced John Bramton to keep Lucifer.'

Little escaped Mr Skinner's notice. He would never have obtained the position he held, and the substance he possessed, had it not been for his faculty of close observation. It was a maxim with him that information, however trivial, was always worth picking up. A straw shows which way the wind blows, and racing men are wonderfully quick at catching a hint that will be of use to them in their vocation. Many a trifle like this had, when interpreted, helped Mr Skinner to make money. The mere fact of Lucifer not being offered for sale would suggest that the stable set store upon him; and his trainer freely acknowledged that they were sanguine about his turning out promising. But the bookmaker looked upon it that he had caught a clue to something more than that—a clue to what, he had no

idea—but what motive had John Bramton in excepting this colt from his ap-
proaching sale? Damocles and Whitechapel he could understand, that was by
the advice of his trainer, and it was quite
likely that Bramton, after tasting the
sweets of winning, might think that there
was more money to be made by running
Damocles than selling him. But these
reasons did not apply to Lucifer. Stubber
had most distinctly said that it was by no
advice of his that the colt was kept, and
whether he could win or not was yet to
be seen. A shrewd, suspicious man, but
with no great faith in anybody but himself, Mr Skinner turned this puzzle over
and over in his mind as he walked his
hack home to his lodgings.

Lord Ranksborow had taken a much
more correct estimate than his commissioner. True he had had many more
opportunities of seeing the owner of
Temple Rising than his agent; but
Skinner had fallen into the mistake that,
because Bramton was simple and ignor-

ant about the affairs of the turf, he was
equally simple and foolish in other matters.
Lord Ranksborow had divined this; he
saw that Bramton was a man who usually
acted on his own judgment, and that if
he sought advice eagerly about the disposal of these horses, it was not so much
that he meant to take it, but really to
learn the worth of and how to make the
most of the property that had so unex-
pectedly fallen into his hands. Could
they but have known the real state of
the case, and seen Mr Pecker's last
letter, both Mr Skinner and the Earl
would have been not a little astonished.
However, Mr Skinner could make no
more of his puzzle at present than that
Lord Ranksborow must have been the
person who had inspired Bramton to
keep Lucifer, and yet, somehow, he felt
that was not the true solution. First
of all, the Earl usually confided to him
any piece of turf strategy which he had
planned; and secondly, what object could
his patron have in the retention of

Lucifer? According to Stubber, they had never as yet fairly tried the colt, and their estimate of his merits was therefore conjectural. He was not a youngster for whom a long price had been paid, as in the case of Damocles, nor had he been talked about, nor his advent on a racecourse expected with all the interest and curiosity that had attended that of the latter. He doubted, indeed, whether Lucifer's career as yet was not a matter of complete indifference to Lord Ranksborow, and then asked himself again, angrily, 'What the deuce made John Bramton keep that colt?' Mr Skinner had passed much time, and not altogether unprofitably, in working out knotty points of this description.

There were two other men also returning from the Heath after watching the gallops that morning, but these young persons were not riding, but trusting to their own legs to bring them back to town.

' It's a little hard, Sim,' said the younger

of the two, a fresh-complexioned young
fellow of about twenty ; 'those horses will
fetch a pot of money next week, and
by rights I ought to have the biggest
part of it.'

'If what you tell me is true,' replied
his companion, a sharp, wizened, preter-
naturally old young man, 'it is rather
rough. Richard Bramton must have left
a good bit of money behind him, and
if what you say is true, and you really
are his son, he ought to have done something for you ; but nobody ever heard
that Dick Bramton was married.'

'Well, it was many years ago, and I
don't suppose he was much older than
I am now, and then he and mother soon
parted. They couldn't get along together.
I don't want to say a word against her,
poor thing, but you see, Sim, she had a
temper, and what's worse, she couldn't
leave the bottle alone. It's not much
wonder Bramton couldn't get on with
her.'

'You will excuse my asking a question,'

said Simon Napper, ' I suppose you've got proof of this marriage ? '

' No, I haven't ; but mother always declared she was married.'

Mr Napper was an attorney's clerk, and his profession taught him to put but little faith in an assertion that could not be corroborated.

' And you've never been called by any other name than Robbins ? '

' No,' returned the other. ' When my father and mother separated, it was a condition that she should resume her maiden name, and live away from New-market. He allowed her all he could at first, and latterly made her a fairly liberal allowance ; but a little before her death he gave her a lump sum down.'

' I see,' said Mr Napper ; ' he capital-ised the allowance, and made it over to her to do as she liked with.'

' Not altogether,' replied Robbins ; ' she could only touch the interest during her life, but she could will it to whom she liked.'

'And she, I suppose, left it to you?'

'Yes; but what was the good of three thousand pounds?'

'Good of it?' returned Mr Napper; 'why, it was enough to start any man with a head on his shoulders in any business. Why, your father Dick Bramton began with nothing, and he left, according to all accounts, a pretty good pile behind him.'

'Yes,' returned Robbins; 'but then he had such luck. Now, I never had any luck. If I back a horse, it's sure to break down or do something awkward— go the wrong side of the post, or be disqualified for foul riding.'

'Strikes me, Master Tom, there was just this difference between yourself and your father,— he had a head on his shoulders, and mentally you've not. Didn't he ever take any notice of you? Didn't he ever do anything for you?'

'No; I never knew he was my father even till after his death. My mother was very ill then, and she told me the story, and vowed that she was really married to him. She said she had kept the secret, as she had promised, and would have still kept it had it not been for his death. A few weeks later, poor soul, and she followed him.'

'And he never did anything for you?'

'Well,' replied Tom Robbins, in a somewhat shamefaced way, 'you know some three years ago, just about the time you were articled, you were astonished at my being taken into the bank. Well, mother said a very old friend of hers had managed that for her, and given her a liberal cheque for me to get a regular rig out with. As you know, it wasn't many months before I got the sack. Mother was in a great taking about it; said I'd quarrelled with the best friend I had, who was very angry, and declared he'd do nothing more for me. Now I don't know for certain, but I think that was my father.'

'Most likely,' rejoined Mr Napper.

' Well, you *were* a fool, though, of course, you didn't know how big a one at the time. Nothing is more likely than that you would have come into a big slice of Dick Bramton's money if you had only kept straight. I suppose you've made a tidy hole in that three thousand pounds your mother left you ? '

' Yes,' replied Tom Robbins ; ' I'm such an unlucky devil, I never win.'

Mr Tom Robbins was a weak-kneed, foolish young man, with no backbone to his character, with idle and vicious propensities, never likely to do any good for himself in this world, and who, had he had the slightest idea of his claim upon Richard Bramton, would have endeavoured to batten on him like a horse-leech. The very few people who knew anything about this episode in Richard Bramton's earlier life would, I fancy, have put a very different complexion upon it. They would rather have laughed at the idea of there having been any marriage, and pronounced Dick Bramton thoroughly

justified in not binding himself for life
to a woman of such violent temper and
intemperate habits as Mary Robbins.
Moreover, it might have been very
plausibly argued that, if she had marriage lines to show, such a headstrong
woman as Mary Robbins would never
have acquiesced in abandoning her position as a wife. Further, scandal rather
credited her with being but a light o'
love at the best.

'Well, I did think I should have taken
something under his will,' continued Tom,
after a short pause. 'As I've never heard
from the lawyers anything about it, nor,
indeed, what his will was, I suppose
there is nothing for me. If I could only
find that certificate, I suppose, I should
come into all.'

'That don't follow at all,' rejoined
Mr Napper. 'Richard Bramton could
leave his money to whom he pleased, and
from all I've heard, Dick Bramton was
just the man to leave a son out in the
cold who displeased him.'

'But it's deuced unfair!' cried Tom, in a lachrymose tone, 'that everything should go to an uncle whom I've never seen. There might be something left to me; there might be a recommendation to my Uncle John to lend me a hand. I should like to see that will.'

'You are perfectly right there,' rejoined Mr Napper; 'always see a will in which you think there is any possibility of your being interested. It only costs a shilling, and it's worth the trouble and outlay. On the off chance, I don't suppose anything will come of it, but, as I said before, it's worth spending a shilling over.'

'I'll do it,' said Tom; 'and now I must go home and write my report.'

Mr Robbins at present held the responsible position of reporter at headquarters to a London sporting paper, and though so far he had never electrified its readers by any striking intelligence, yet he managed to get through his work well enough to retain his situation.

'He'll never come to any good,' thought Simon Napper, as he mused over the above conversation. 'She didn't like to acknowledge it, no doubt, but depend upon it, his mother never *was* married; and a self-made, reliant man like Richard Bramton would have no patience with a feeble, feckless fool like that. Tom little thought when he was kicked out of that situation, and used to be swaggering and vapouring about what a fast life he had led in London, that he was doing this under the nose of his own father, and a father too, with a pot of money to leave.'

CHAPTER XV.

THE JULY STAKES.

THE racing world were gathered together at the back of the ditch for the celebration of one of the pleasantest meetings of the year. After the roar of Epsom and the crowd of Ascot the comparative quiet of the July Meeting is most enjoyable. Held in the midst of summer, and favoured as a rule with splendid weather, it enjoys also another distinct privilege—there is licence in the matter of dress. On the Royal Heath fashion demands the showiest costumes, and is inexorable about the chimney-pot on the part of the male sex. At Newmarket you may do as you please in the matter

of attire, and defy the fierce rays of the
sun as you so will it. Amongst those
who had come for the sport were a considerable section who were quite as much
attracted by the sales. To many men
the looking over thoroughbred stock, the
talking over how the youngsters are
bred, the arguing about the different
strains of blood, and, above all, how the
prices for which the youngsters are sold
coincides with their own judgment, is
quite as interesting as the racing itself;
then there were the buyers always ex-
pecting to draw a prize out of that most
capricious of lucky-bags, a yearling sale.
Often as they have given long prices
only to find that the youngsters who
had fallen to the auctioneer's hammer
for a thousand and upwards were never
destined to realise the high hopes enter-
tained of them, still, carried away by the
grand looks of some colt, or of a strain
of blood that they peculiarly fancy, they
take one more ticket in Fortune's wheel,
only to find once more that,—

> 'Legs are not steel, and steel is bent;
> Legs are not rocks, and rocks are rent,'

and that the high price purchase succumbs to the exigencies of training.

The sale of the late Richard Bramton's horses was not calculated to attract undue attention. Good, useful horses they were, and likely to sell well; but everybody knew that 'the pick of the basket,' Damocles, was not to be put up. That Lucifer also was reserved was noticed only by a few old hands. The colt had never run, and therefore was almost unknown by name to the racegoers; but amongst the few people whose attention it did attract were Lord Ranksborow, Mr James Noel, and Mr Simon Napper. For the first time since that memorable visit to Epsom in his youth, John Bramton had been fairly goaded into appearing on a racecourse. He had no idea of being present at Newmarket, or indeed any other race meeting, but the feminine pressure brought to bear had proved too strong for him.

In spite of his first curt refusal, accompanied by the comments that he had never heard such preposterous nonsense, and that Newmarket was no place for ladies, Mrs Bramton and her daughters returned again and again to the charge. Those comments of John Bramton had been injudicious. He had advanced reasons for his refusal, which, as Lord Chancellor Thurloe said, 'you should never do.' It was speedily proved to him, on the testimony of the Ladies Cuxwold, that there was nothing at all preposterous in the idea, that ladies *did* go to Newmarket, and that very jolly it was.

'Quite lovely!' said Lady Emily. 'Just a sailor hat and a muslin dress; and you take a big hamper in the carriage, and picnic on the grass; and you can get about, and haven't all the horrid crowd of Ascot. I only wish papa would take us; but he says he can't afford a cottage this year.'

Supported by these authorities, Mrs

Bramton and her daughters gave the head of the house no peace. He felt that he would have to yield. Mrs Bramton and the girls usually carried their point at last, and, therefore, John Bramton felt he might as well give in as prolong the struggle. Added to which, Lucy privately urged that she ought to be allowed to see her own horses run, more especially as she was in a position, as she said, 'to pay for the lark.' So it had been resolved that the whole party were to make their racing *début* on the Heath, under the auspices of Lord Ranksborow.

One trifling difficulty had presented itself. In the first instance, Lord Ranksborow had suggested a hack to Mr Bramton, but about this the master of Temple Rising was very positive. If it were not possible to see horse-racing except by getting on a horse, then he would contrive to do without that sight.

The Earl laughed, and speedily reassured him, and said, 'that, upon the whole, a good roomy carriage would probably suit the whole party much better,' and re-assured for the present about Damocles, the Earl promised to act as a mentor in some sort, to see that their carriage was placed in a proper position, etc., and cordially accepted an invitation to come and pick a bit with them at luncheon time.

A favourite expression of Mr Bramton's was, ' I never go in for things by halves ; ' and, now, having gone in for racing, he was determined to act up to his favourite maxim. He sent down a roomy barouche and a pair of job-horses from London, and as for hampers, their size and number gave the idea that Bramton contemplated asking half the Heath to lunch with him. He really was of a hospitable disposition, but this result was principally due to the absurd idea he had conceived of his own importance as the *soi-disant* owner of Damocles. He really did conceive that many of the leading patrons of the turf desired to make his acquaintance, and would probably have expected to be at

once elected a member of the Jockey
Club, had he remembered that such a
body existed. His neighbours at Temple
Rising had a little fostered this idea.
He ignored the well-known axiom, 'You
may be a big man in the country,
and a very small one in the metropolis.'
Newmarket *is* the metropolis of the
turf.

The Miss Bramtons experienced much
difficulty in restraining their father in the
matter of dress. True to his great prin-
ciple of not going in for things by halves,
Mr Bramton was excessively anxious to
attire himself as a genuine racing man.
How these arrayed themselves he did not
know, but his own idea was evolved from
his inner consciousness and a hazy re-
collection of the Hill at Espom, and, but
for the control of his daughters, John
Bramton's get-up would have been very
striking. He had doubts as to whether
top-boots were not a *sine qua non* for a
professed owner of racehorses, but this
was finally compromised for a pair of

extremely tight-fitting, horsey-looking cord
trousers and a white hat, which the girls
felt it was useless to combat, and, besides,
there was nothing remarkable in that,
but a dust-coloured coat of very pronounced colour was the occasion of a long
struggle, eventually terminating in the
defeat of Matilda and Lucy. Mr Bramton vowed he would go to Newmarket
in that salmon-tinted garment, or he
would not go at all; and, thus attired,
armed with a Brobdignagian pair of race
glasses, made his first appearance on
Newmarket Heath.

Mr Bramton was not a little disappointed at the aspect of Newmarket.
True to that one racing reminiscence of
his juvenile days, he had pictured to himself all the knock-'em-downs, cocoa-nuts,
nigger minstrels, and the other eccentric
artists that swarm about the Hill at
Epsom. The absence of this element
depressed him.

' Aristocratic, my dears!' he exclaimed;
' but don't you think it's just a leetle dull ?

And if these are the swells, all I can say is they don't dress up to the mark.'

And here Mr Bramton pulled up his shirt-collar, as much as to say that he, at all events, was not liable to that accusation.

'That flame-coloured garment of papa's will be our ruin!' whispered Miss Matilda to her sister. 'What a happy thought that was of yours, Lucy, about the gloves.'

Lucy had ingeniously kidnapped a very bright-coloured pair of gloves that her father had elected to wear at the last moment, substituting a more sombre-hued pair in their place.

And now the horses go leisurely down to the post for the Julys.

'Oh! papa,' exclaimed Matilda, 'what a hideous jacket yours is! You really must change it.'

Once more did Lucy, thoroughly agreeing with her sister on this point, inwardly vow that next year should see Damocles run in prettier colours.

But the babel of the ring is stilled, the

flag falls, and the field are away for the Julys. Hardly a sound breaks the soft summer air, and every eye is strained upon that cluster of gay jackets so rapidly nearing the spectators. The thud of the advancing hoofs now falls distinctly on the ear, followed by the cry of ' Prize-fighter wins ! ' ' Harlequin wins ! ' Mr Bramton feels his head turning. He is fumbling with his glasses, and, has lost sight of the horses, when suddenly rings through the air the clear, distinct tones of Lord Ranksborow,—

'A hundred to ten on Damocles ! Damocles wins !—wins in a canter ! '

A couple of minutes more, up goes the number, and it is evident the Earl's verdict has been confirmed.

' Let me congratulate you, Mr Bramton,' said Lord Ranksborow, as he raised his hat and reined up his horse by the side of the carriage. ' I don't know what the judge's verdict may be, but I'm quite convinced that your horse won easily. I am going to take the liberty of asking you to

give an old friend of mine some lunch.
Let me introduce you to Mr Flood.'

Alec raised his hat, while a little hand
was extended from the carriage to him,
and Lucy exclaimed,—

'Mr Flood and I are old acquaintances.
I trust you recollect me ?'

'Not likely that I should forget you,
Miss Bramton,' replied Alec, as he shook
hands. 'I have often wondered whether
we should meet again, and little thought it
would be here. I don't very often trouble
a racecourse, though I might have known
it was not an unlikely place to meet you.'

She could hardly have explained why,
but Lucy felt a little nettled at this remark ; and yet she had been dying to pay
this visit to Newmarket. Her horse was
successful, and everything promised to
make the day *couleur de rose.* She
wanted to meet Flood, but she was conscious that she would rather have met
him anywhere else.

'There you are wrong,' replied Lucy.
'I have never been on a racecourse be-

fore, and if it hadn't been for my poor uncle's death, should probably have not been here now ; but Damocles, you know, was his horse, and we were all anxious to see him win just once.'

'Of course ; I understand now. By the way, I remember hearing that the stud became your father's property. I must congratulate you, Mr Bramton.'

'Very good of you, I'm sure. Yes ; they tell me that horse of mine is a regular "sneezer." At all events, he keeps win- ning, which is satisfactory. But just give your horse to one of the men there to hold, and come up on the box and have some lunch.'

'Don't you think, Mr Flood, we have the most hideous jacket there is re- gistered ? Papa, you really must change it.'

'Good heavens! don't be so rash, Miss Bramton,' cried Lord Ranksborow. 'You can't do more than win. Any old race- goer will tell you, as I do, that to change your jacket is to change your luck.'

'Poor Uncle Dick used to say that they might not be pretty, that wasn't in his way; what he liked about them was that they were good to see.'

'Ridiculous!' exclaimed John Bramton. 'Here am I, with a spic-span new pair of Voigtlander's glasses, and I'm blessed if I could ever see 'em at any part of the race.'

'There is a little knack in distinguishing colours through a race-glass,' said Ranksborow; 'you will soon get into it. And now, Mr Bramton, you must come with me, and walk across and say something pretty to Stubber. Quite the correct thing, I assure you, and I must say he has done your colt every justice.'

'Oh! well,' said Mr Bramton, 'I shall be only too happy, if it's the correct thing. I'm always anxious to do the correct thing, your lordship.'

The Earl had given his hack over to his groom while he made his modest lunch at the Bramtons' carriage. Making a sign to the lad to follow him, he and his en-

tertainer now walked off in search of the
trainer, upon meeting whom Mr Bramton
was destined to be still further astonished. Lord Ranksborow shook hands
with Stubber, congratulated him upon
landing the Julys, and complimented him
upon the condition of his horse, winding
up by saying,—

'I have brought Mr Bramton to talk
to you.'

'Hope you're satisfied, sir,' said Stubber,
as he touched his hat.

'It's the correct thing to be affable;
all the swells do it, I see,' muttered Mr
Bramton, *sotto voce*, 'so here goes. How
d'ye do, Stubber? Very glad to see you,
Stubber. You do Damocles great credit,
or Damocles does you, which is it? 'Pon
my word, I don't know; but if you'll just
come across to my carriage we'll have a
glass of champagne over this.'

'Yes, and a right good glass, too,'
chimed in the Earl. 'You ought to
drink Mr Bramton's health on his first
appearance on the Heath,' and with these

words the Earl signalled to his groom to bring up his hack, and left Mr Bramton and his trainer to celebrate their victory.

'Have you heard lately from Captain Cuxwold?' asked Lucy, as her father and Lord Ranksborow left the carriage.

'Not very lately,' replied Flood. 'But why don't you apply to headquarters?' and Alec jerked his head in the direction of the retreating Earl.

'I was wondering only the other day,' replied Lucy, 'whether he was connected with the Ranksborow family.'

'Pretty closely,' rejoined Flood, laughing; 'he is a son. I wonder you didn't guess that long ago. Surely you knew he was the Honourable Captain Cuxwold, at Cairo?'

'No,' replied Lucy. 'I only knew that he was Captain Cuxwold; then, again, we have only known Lord Ranksborow and his family quite lately, and I must plead guilty to being supremely ignorant about the peerage. It was only the other day that I knew Lord Ranksborow's family name. But you have not answered my question?'

'I heard from Jack not long ago. Of course you know he was up with Sir Gerald Graham at Suakim, and you must have read in the papers what the fighting was like up there.'

'Terrible,' rejoined Lucy; 'but I had no idea Captain Cuxwold was in the midst of all that carnage.'

'Yes; it was pretty hard fighting. These Arabs are splendid fellows, and fight like wild cats; but they are likely to see plenty more of it before all is over. We've sent Gordon to Khartoum, and he is besieged there. We are in honour bound to go to his relief, and, what's more, the outcry in the country is getting so strong that Government cannot put off sending an expedition much longer. It doesn't much matter where they start from, but there'll be bitter fighting in the desert between that and Khartoum. But see, they are going down for another race.

Do you take much interest in this sort of thing ? '

'Yes, I do,' she replied, as she stood up in the carriage, with flushed cheeks and sparkling eyes, though how she could look so excited, considering how little she knew about it, was singular.   It is possible she was thinking more about the perils of the Soudan than the mimic warfare of the racecourse.   'How I do wish we had a horse of our own running in this.'

Alec Flood had never been suspected of taking any very great interest in turf matters, but this afternoon he spent watching the racing closely from the box of the Bramtons' carriage.

END OF VOL. I.

COLSTON AND COMPANY, PRINTERS, EDINBURGH.

www.ingramcontent.com/pod-product-compliance
Lightning Source LLC
Chambersburg PA
CBHW030804020726
47499CB00006B/1758